"It's only sex ... all I can give...

Sawyer's words emerged as a rough growl because he didn't want to say them.

To his surprise, Honey merely nodded, then repeated, "Only sex. That's probably for the best."

He lifted her into his arms. "So be it. At least we're agreed."

She clutched at his shoulders and she gasped. "But...it's late."

"If you think I'm going to wait one second more, you're mistaken." He lowered her to the mattress, then followed her down. In one movement he used his knee to open her slender thighs.

"If you'd gotten away today, I'd have come after you," he murmured, settling between her legs. "I had to know what it'd be like to have you under me, naked...mine."

She stared up at him, then with a moan she pulled him down so their mouths met—open and hot. Sawyer gave up any hope of slowing down. He'd only known her a few short days. *But heaven help him, he felt as if he'd been waiting a lifetime for her....*

Dear Reader,

I am so very excited and pleased to bring you the first book in my new miniseries, THE BUCKHORN BROTHERS. From the moment I conceived this idea, I loved each and every one of the big lugs—and there are four of them. To me, men are so complex, so fun and so *different* from us women! How can we not love them?

I've had people write and ask if guys like my fictional heroes really exist. I'm pleased to tell you that, yes, they do. I personally know four of them. I have dibs on one, because we've been married for over twenty-two years now, and like fine wine he gets better every year—so I'm not about to give him up. And the other three—my sons—aren't old enough yet, so hands off!

Next month you'll meet *Morgan* the sheriff (Temptation #790). Look for *Gabe* the heartthrob in August (Temptation #794) and finally, in September, *Jordan* the sweet-talkin' vet will sweep you off your feet (Temptation #798). As you read this series—and hopefully fall in love with my heroes—remember to laugh, remember to keep some ice water handy and please, remember to believe....

All my best to all of you!

Lori Foster

P.S. You can write to me at P.O. Box 854, Ross, Ohio, 45061

Lori Foster
SAWYER

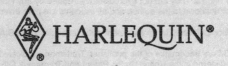

HARLEQUIN®

TORONTO • NEW YORK • LONDON
AMSTERDAM • PARIS • SYDNEY • HAMBURG
STOCKHOLM • ATHENS • TOKYO • MILAN • MADRID
PRAGUE • WARSAW • BUDAPEST • AUCKLAND

If you purchased this book without a cover you should be aware
that this book is stolen property. It was reported as "unsold and
destroyed" to the publisher, and neither the author nor the
publisher has received any payment for this "stripped book."

To my son, Aaron.

Every step of the way, even as a small child,
you've been one of the most unique,
independent people I know. And one of the finest.
I wish I could claim responsibility for that,
but the truth is, all I've done is love you—
and that has always been so easy to do.
To say I'm proud would be an
unbelievable understatement. But hey,
what the heck? I *am* so proud,
and I love you very much.

ISBN 0-373-25886-0

SAWYER

Copyright © 2000 by Lori Foster.

All rights reserved. Except for use in any review, the reproduction or
utilization of this work in whole or in part in any form by any electronic,
mechanical or other means, now known or hereafter invented, including
xerography, photocopying and recording, or in any information storage
or retrieval system, is forbidden without the written permission of the
publisher, Harlequin Enterprises Limited, 225 Duncan Mill Road,
Don Mills, Ontario, Canada M3B 3K9.

All characters in this book have no existence outside the imagination of
the author and have no relation whatsoever to anyone bearing the same
name or names. They are not even distantly inspired by any individual
known or unknown to the author, and all incidents are pure invention.

This edition published by arrangement with Harlequin Books S.A.

® and TM are trademarks of the publisher. Trademarks indicated with
® are registered in the United States Patent and Trademark Office, the
Canadian Trade Marks Office and in other countries.

Visit us at www.eHarlequin.com

Printed in U.S.A.

_____ 1 _____

ONE MINUTE he'd been reveling in the late afternoon sun, feeling the sweat dry on his shoulders and neck before he could wipe it away.

In the next instant, she was there.

He'd just glanced over at his son, Casey, only fifteen, but working as hard as any man, tall and strong and determined. His smile was filled with incredible pride.

The last two weekends he'd been caught up with patients, and he'd missed working outside with Casey, enjoying the fresh air, using his hands and body until the physical strain tired him.

Summer scents were heavy in the air, drifting to him as he layered another replacement board on the fence and hammered it in. A warm, humid breeze stirred his hair, bringing with it the promise of a harsh evening storm. He'd inhaled deeply, thinking how perfect his life was.

Then his son shouted, "Holy sh—ah, heck!" catching Sawyer's attention.

Not knowing what to expect, Sawyer turned in the direction Casey pointed his hammer and disbelief filled him as a rusted sedan, moving at breakneck speed, came barreling down the gravel road bordering their property. The turn at the bottom, hugging the

Kentucky hills, was sharp; the car would never make it.

Sawyer got a mere glimpse of a pale, wide-eyed female face behind the wheel before, tires squealing, gravel flying, the car came right through the fence he'd just repaired, splintering wood and scattering nails, forcing him to leap for cover. Sheer momentum sent the car airborne for a few feet before it hit the grassy ground with a loud thump and was propelled forward several more feet to slide hood first into a narrow cove of the lake. The front end was submerged, hissing and bubbling, while the trunk and back wheels still rested on solid land, leaving the car at a crazy tilt.

Both Sawyer and Casey stood frozen for several seconds, stunned by what had happened, before ungluing their feet and rushing to the edge of the small cove. Without hesitation, Casey waded waist-deep into the water and peered in the driver's window. "It's a girl!"

Sawyer pushed him aside and leaned down.

His breath caught and held. "Girl" wasn't exactly an apt description of the unconscious woman inside. In a heartbeat, he took in all her features, scanning her from head to toes. As a doctor, he looked for signs of injury, but as a man, he appreciated how incredibly, utterly feminine she was. He guessed her to be in her mid-twenties. Young, a tiny woman, but definitely full grown.

The window was thankfully open, giving him easy access to her, but water rapidly washed into the car, almost covering her shins. Silently cursing himself and his masculine, knee-jerk reaction to her, he told Casey,

"Go to the truck and call Gabe at the house. Tell him to meet us out front."

Casey hurried off while Sawyer considered the situation. The woman was out cold, her head slumped over the steering wheel, her body limp. The back seat of the car was filled with taped cardboard boxes and luggage, some of which had tumbled forward, landing awkwardly against her. A few open crates had dumped, and items—bric-a-brac, books and framed photos—were strewn about. It was obvious she'd been packed up for a long trip—or a permanent one.

Sawyer reached for her delicate wrist and was rewarded to feel a strong pulse. Her skin was velvety smooth, warm to the touch. He carefully placed her hand back in her lap, keeping it away from the icy cold water.

It took some doing, but he got the driver's door wedged open. If the car had surged a little deeper into the lake, he never would have managed it. More water flooded in. The woman moaned and turned her head, pushing away from the steering wheel, then dropping forward again. Her easy, unconscious movements assured Sawyer she had no spinal or neck injuries. After moving the fallen objects away from her, he carefully checked her slender arms, slipping his fingers over her warm flesh, gently flexing each elbow, wrist and shoulder. He drew his hands over her jeans-clad legs beneath the water, but again found no injuries. Her lips parted and she groaned, a rasping, almost breathless sound of pain. Frowning, Sawyer examined the swelling bump on her head. He didn't like it that she was still out, and her skin felt a little too warm, almost feverish.

Casey came to a skidding, sloshing halt beside him, sending waves to lap at Sawyer's waist. His gaze was narrowed with concern on the woman's face. "Gabe offered to bring you your bag, but I told him I'd call him back if you needed it." He spoke in a whisper, as if afraid of disturbing her. "We're taking her to the house with us, aren't we?"

"Looks like." If she didn't come to on the way to the house, he'd get her over to the hospital. But that was a good hour away, and most people in Buckhorn chose him over the hospital anyway, unless the situation was truly severe. And even then, it was generally his call.

He'd decide what to do after he determined the extent of her injuries. But first things first; he needed to get her out of the car and away from the debilitating effects of the cold water and hot sun.

Luckily, they weren't that far away from the house. He owned fifty acres, thick with trees and scrub bushes and wildflowers. The lake, long and narrow like a river, bordered the back of his property for a long stretch of shore. The ten acres surrounding the house and abutting the lake were kept mowed, and though it couldn't be called an actual road, there was a worn dirt path where they often brought the truck to the cove to fish or swim. Today they'd driven down to make repairs to a worn fence.

A crooked smile tipped up one side of his mouth. Thanks to the lady, the repairs to the fence were now more necessary than ever.

Sawyer carefully slid one arm beneath her legs, the

other behind the small of her back. Her head tipped toward him, landing softly on his bare, sweaty shoulder. Her hair was a deep honey blond with lighter sun streaks framing her face. It smelled of sunshine and woman, and he instinctively breathed in the scent, letting it fill his lungs. Her hair was long enough to drag across the car seat as he lifted her out. "Grab her keys and purse, then get the shirt I left by the fence." He needed to cover her, and not only to counter the chill of the lake water.

He was almost ashamed to admit it, even to himself, but he'd noticed right off that her white T-shirt was all but transparent with the dousing she'd taken. And she wasn't wearing a bra.

He easily shook that observation from his mind.

Even with her clothes soaked, the woman weighed next to nothing, but still it was an effort to climb the small embankment out of the lake without jarring her further. She'd lost one thin sandal in the wreck, and now the other fell off with a small splash. The mud squished beneath Sawyer's boots, making for unsure footing. Casey scrambled out ahead, then caught at Sawyer's elbow, helping to steady him. Once they were all on the grassy embankment, Casey ran off to follow the rest of his instructions, but was back in a flash with the shirt, which he helped Sawyer arrange around her shoulders. Sawyer kept her pressed close to his chest, preserving her privacy and saving his son from major embarrassment.

"You want me to drive?" Walking backward, Casey managed to keep his gaze on the woman and avoid tripping.

"Yeah, but slowly. No unnecessary bumps, okay?" Casey was still learning the rudiments of changing gears, and he used any excuse to get behind the wheel.

"No problem, I'll just..." His voice trailed off as the woman stirred, lifting one limp hand to her forehead.

Sawyer stopped, holding her securely in his arms. He stared down at her face, waiting for her to regain complete awareness, strangely anticipating her reaction. "Easy now."

Her lashes were thick and dark brown tipped with gold and they fluttered for a moment before her eyes slowly opened—and locked on his. Deep, deep blue, staring into him, only inches away.

Sawyer became aware of several things at once: her soft, accelerated breath on his throat, the firmness of her slim thighs on his bare arm, her breasts pressing through the damp cotton of her shirt against his ribs. He could feel the steady drumming of her heartbeat, and the way her body now stiffened the tiniest bit. He felt a wave of tingling awareness shudder through his body, from his chest all the way to his thighs. His reaction to her was out of proportion, considering the circumstances and his usual demeanor. He was a physician, for God's sake, and didn't, in the normal course of things, even notice a woman as a woman when medical treatment was required.

Right now, he couldn't help but notice. Holding this particular woman was somehow altogether different. So often, he put aside his tendencies as a man in deference to those of a doctor; being a doctor was such an enormous part of him. But now he found it difficult to separate the two. The doctor was present, concerned

for her health and determined to give her the best of his
care. But the man was also there, acutely aware of her
femininity and unaccountably responding to it in a
very basic way. He'd never faced such a pickle before,
and he felt equal parts confusion, curiosity and something entirely too close to embarrassment. For a moment while they stared at each other, it was so silent, he
imagined he could hear her thoughts.

Then she slugged him.

Though she had no strength at all and her awkward
blow barely grazed him, he was so taken by surprise he
nearly dropped her. While Casey stood there gawking,
making no effort to help, Sawyer struggled to maintain
his hold and his balance with a squirming woman in
his arms.

Out of sheer self-preservation, he lowered her bare
feet to the ground—then had to catch her again as she
swayed and almost crumpled. She would have fallen if
both he and Casey hadn't grabbed hold of some part of
her, but she still made the feeble effort to shrug them
both away.

"No!" she said in a rough, whispering croak, as if
her panicked voice could do no better.

"Hey, now," Sawyer crooned, trying the tone he'd
often heard his brother Jordan use when talking to a
sick or frightened animal. "You're okay."

She tried to swing at him again, he ducked back, and
she whirled in a clumsy circle, stopping when her
small fist made contact with Casey's shoulder. Casey
jumped a good foot, unhurt but startled, then rubbed
his arm.

Enough was enough.

Sawyer wrapped his arms around her from behind, both supporting and restraining her. "Shh. It's okay," he said, over and over again. She appeared somewhat disoriented, possibly from the blow to her head. "Settle down now before you hurt yourself."

His words only prompted more struggles, but her movements were ineffectual.

"Lady," he whispered very softly, "you're terrorizing my son."

With a gasp, she glanced up at Casey, who looked young and very strong, maybe bursting with curiosity, but in no way terrorized.

Sawyer smiled, then continued in calm, even tones. "Listen to me now, okay? Your car landed in our lake and we fished you out. You were unconscious. It's probable you have a concussion, on top of whatever else ails you."

"Let me go."

Her body shook from head to toe, a mixture of shock and illness, Sawyer decided, feeling that her skin was definitely too hot. "If I let you go you'll fall flat on your face. That or try to hit my boy again."

If anything, she panicked more, shaking her head wildly. "No..."

After glaring at Sawyer, Casey held both arms out to his sides. "Hey, lady, I'm not hurt. I'm fine." His neck turned red, but his voice was as calm and soothing as his father's. "Really. Dad just wants to help you."

"Who are you?"

She wasn't talking to Casey now. All her attention seemed to be on staying upright. Even with Sawyer's help, she was wobbly. He gently tightened his hold, keeping her close and hindering her futile movements. "Sawyer Hudson, ma'am. I'm the man who owns this property. Me and my brothers. As I said, you landed in my lake. But I'm also a doctor and I'm going to help you." He waited for a name, for a reciprocal introduction, but none was forthcoming.

"Just...just let me go."

Slowly, still maintaining his careful hold on her, he turned them both until they faced the lake. "You see your car? It's not going anywhere, honey. Not without a tow truck and some major repairs."

She gasped, and her entire body went rigid. "You know my name."

He didn't understand her, but he understood shock. "Not yet, but I will soon. Now..." He paused as her face washed clean of color and she pressed one hand to her mouth. Sawyer quickly lowered her to her knees, still supporting her from behind. "You going to be sick?"

"Oh, God."

"Now just take a few deep breaths. That's it." To Casey, he said, "Go get the water," and his son took off at a sprint, his long legs eating up the ground.

Sawyer turned back to the woman and continued in his soft, soothing tone. "You feel sick because of the blow to your head. It's all right." At least, he thought that was the cause. She also felt feverish, and that couldn't be attributed to a concussion. After a moment of watching her gulp down deep breaths, he asked, "Any better?"

She nodded. Her long fair hair hung nearly to the ground, hiding her face like a silky, tangled curtain. He wrapped it around his hand and pulled it away so he could see her clearly. Her eyes were closed, her mouth pinched. Casey rushed up with the water bottle, and Sawyer held it to her lips. "Take a few sips. There you go. Real slow, now." He watched her struggling for control and wished for some way to lessen the nausea for her. "Let's get you out of this hot sun, okay? I can get you more comfortable in a jiffy."

"I need my car."

Didn't she remember crashing into the water? Sawyer frowned. "Let me take you to my house, get you dried off and give your belly a chance to settle. I'll have one of my brothers pull your car out and see about having it towed to the garage to be cleaned..."

"No!"

Getting somewhat exasperated, Sawyer leaned around until he could meet her gaze. Her lush bottom lip trembled, something he couldn't help but make note of. He chided himself. "No, what?"

She wouldn't look at him, still doing her best to shy away. "No, don't have it towed."

"Okay." She appeared ready to drop, her face now flushed, her lips pale. He didn't want to push her, to add to her confusion. His first priority was determining how badly she might be hurt.

He tried a different tack. "How about coming to my house and getting dry? You can use the phone, call someone to give you a hand."

He watched her nostrils flare as she sucked in a slow, labored breath—then started coughing. Sawyer loosened his hold to lift her arms above her head, supporting her and making it easier for her to breathe. Once she'd calmed, he wrapped her close again, giving her his warmth as she continued to shiver.

She swallowed hard and asked, "Why? Why would you want to help me? I don't believe you."

Leaning back on his heels, he realized she was truly terrified. Not just of the situation, of being with total strangers and being hurt and sick, but of him specifically. It floored him, and doubled his curiosity. He was a doctor, respected throughout the community, known for his calm and understanding demeanor. Women never feared him, they came to him for help.

Looking over her head to Casey, seeing the mirrored confusion on his son's face, Sawyer tried to decide what to do next. She helped to make up his mind.

"If...if you let me go, I'll give you money."

He hesitated only two seconds before saying, "Casey, go start the truck." Whatever else ailed her, she was terrified and alone and hurt. The mystery of her fear could be solved later.

She stiffened again and her eyes squeezed tight. He heard her whisper, "*No.*"

Determined now, he lifted her to her feet and started her forward, moving at a slow, easy pace so she wouldn't stumble. "'Fraid so. You're in no condition to be on your own."

"What are you going to do?"

A better question was what did she *think* he was going to do. But he didn't ask it, choosing instead to give her an option. "My house or the hospital, take your pick. But I'm not leaving you here alone."

She took two more dragging steps, then held her

head. Her body slumped against his in defeat. "Your...
your house."

Surprised, but also unaccountably pleased, he again
lifted her in his arms. "So you're going to trust me just
a bit after all?"

Her head bumped his chin as she shook it. "Never."

He couldn't help but chuckle. "Lesser of two evils,
huh? Now you know I gotta wonder why the hospital
is off-limits." She winced with each step he took, so he
talked very softly just to distract her. "Did you rob a
bank? Are you a wanted felon?"

"No."

"If I take you in, will someone recognize you?"

"No."

The shirt he'd draped around her was now tangled
at her waist. He tried not to look, but after all, he was
human, a male human, and his gaze went to her
breasts.

She noticed.

Warm color flooded her cheeks, and he rushed to reassure her. "It's all right. Why don't we readjust the
shirt I gave you just a bit?"

She didn't fight him when he loosened his hold
enough to let her legs slip to the ground. She leaned
against him while he pulled the shirt up around her,
slipping her arms through the sleeves. It was an old
faded blue chambray shirt, the sleeves cut short, the
top button missing. He'd often used it for work because it was soft and ragged. She should have looked
ridiculous in it, wearing it like a robe. Instead, she
looked adorable, the shirt in stark contrast to her fragile femininity. The hem hung down to her knees, and it

almost wrapped around her twice. Sawyer shook his head, getting his thoughts back on track once again.

"Better?"

"Yes." She hesitated, clutching the shirt, then whispered, "Thank you."

He watched her face for signs of discomfort as they took the last few steps to the truck. "I'm sorry," he said softly. "You're in pain, aren't you?"

"No, I'm just—"

He interrupted her lie. "Well, lucky for you, I really am a doctor, and for the moment you can keep your name, and why you're so frightened, to yourself. All I want to do right now is help."

Her gaze flicked to his, then away. Sawyer opened the door of the idling truck and helped her inside. He slid in next to her, then laid his palm against her forehead in a gentle touch. "You're running a fever. How long have you been sick?"

Casey put the truck in gear with a rough start that made her wince. He mumbled an apology, then kept the gears smooth after that.

With one hand covering her eyes, she said, "It's... just a cold."

He snorted. Her voice was so raspy, he could barely understand her. "What are your symptoms?"

She shook her head.

"Dizzy?"

"A little."

"Headache? A tightness in your chest?"

"Yes."

Sawyer touched her throat, checking for swollen glands and finding them. "Does this hurt?"

She tried to shrug, but it didn't have the negligent effect she'd probably hoped for. "Some. My throat is sore."

"Trouble breathing?"

She gave a choked half laugh at his persistence. "A little."

"So of course you decided to go for a drive." She opened her mouth to protest, but he said, "Look at me," then gently lifted each eyelid, continuing his examination. She needed to be in bed getting some care. On top of a likely concussion, he suspected an upper respiratory infection, if not pneumonia. Almost on cue, she gave another hoarse, raw cough. "How long have you had that?"

She turned bleary, suspicious eyes his way. "You're a real doctor?"

"Wanna see my bag? All docs have one, you know."

Casey piped up with, "He really is. In fact, he's the only doctor Buckhorn has. Some of the women around here pretend to be sick just to see him." He smiled at her. "You don't need to be afraid."

"Casey, watch the road." The last thing he needed was his son filling her ears with nonsense, even if the nonsense was true. He had a feeling she wouldn't appreciate the local women's antics nearly as much as his brothers or son did. Sawyer treated it all as a lark, because he had no intention of getting involved with any of the women, and they knew it.

He had a respected position in the community and refused to take advantage of their offers. Driving out of the area was always difficult, not to mention time-consuming. He'd had a few long-distance, purely sexual relationships when the fever of lust got to him and he had to have relief. He was a healthy man in every way, and he didn't begrudge himself the occasional weakness due to his sex. But those encounters were never very satisfying, and he sometimes felt it was more trouble than it was worth.

She turned to him, her blue eyes huge again, and worried. She nervously licked at her dry lips. Sawyer felt that damn lick clear down to his gut, and it made him furious, made him wonder if another out-of-town trip wasn't in order. She was a woman, nothing more, nothing less. And at the moment, she looked pale, on the verge of throwing up, and her mood was more surly than not.

So why was he playing at being a primitive, reacting solely on male instincts he hadn't even known he had?

Her worried frown prompted one of his own. "You had a lot of stuff stowed in your back seat. Moving?"

She bit her lip, and her fingers toyed with the tattered edge of the shirt he'd given her, telling him she didn't want to answer his questions. After another bout of coughing where she pressed a fist to her chest and he waited patiently, she whispered, "How do you know my name?"

He lifted one brow. "I don't."

"But..." It was her turn to narrow her eyes, and the blue seemed even more intense in her annoyance, shaded by her thick lashes, accompanied by her flushed cheeks. Then the annoyance turned to pain and she winced, rubbing at her temples.

Compassion filled him. Finding out the truth could wait. For now, she needed his control. There was no faking a fever, or that croupy cough. "You're confused. And no wonder, given how sick you are and that knock on the head you got when your car dove into the lake."

"I'm sorry," she mumbled. "I'll pay for the damage to your fence."

Sawyer didn't reply to that. For some reason, it made him angry. Even the little talking they'd done had weakened her; she was now leaning on him, her eyes closed. But she was concerned for his damn fence? She should have been concerned about her soft hide.

Casey successfully pulled the truck into the yard beneath a huge elm. Gabe sprinted off the porch where he'd been impatiently waiting, and even before Casey killed the engine, Gabe had the truck door open. "What the hell's going on?" Then his eyes widened on the woman, and he whistled.

Sawyer leaned down to her ear. "My baby brother, Gabe," he said by way of introduction. She nodded, but kept silent.

To Gabe, he answered, "A little accident with the lady's car and the lake."

"Casey told me the lake got in her way." Gabe looked her over slowly, his expression inscrutable. "What's wrong with her? And why aren't you taking her to the hospital?"

"Because she doesn't want to go." Sawyer looked down at the woman's bent head. She was shying away from Gabe, which was a phenomenon all in itself. Gabe was the most popular bachelor in Buckhorn. He smiled, and the women went all mushy and adoring, a fact Sawyer and his brothers taunted him with daily and an accolade Gabe accepted with masculine grace.

Of course Gabe wasn't exactly smiling now, too concerned to do so. And the woman wasn't even looking his way. She'd taken one peek at him, then scooted closer to Sawyer, touching him from shoulder to hip.

In almost one movement he lifted her into his lap and stepped out of the truck. He didn't question his motives; he was a doctor and his first instinct was always to care for the injured or sick. She didn't fight him. Instead, she tucked her face close to his throat and held on. Sawyer swallowed hard, moved by some insidious emotion he couldn't name, but knew damn good and well he'd rather not be feeling. Gruffly, he ordered, "Casey, get a bed ready and fetch my bag."

Casey hurried off, but Gabe kept stride beside him. "This is damn strange, Sawyer."

"I know."

"At least tell me if she's hurt bad."

"Mostly sick, I think, but likely a concussion, too." He looked at his youngest brother. "If I can't handle it here, we'll move her to the hospital. But for now, if you're done with the interrogation, I could use your help."

One of Gabe's fair brows shot up, and he crossed his arms over his chest. "Doing what, exactly?"

"The lady had a lot of stuff in the back seat of her car. Can you go get it before it floats away in the lake or gets completely ruined? And get hold of Morgan to have her car towed out." She lifted her head and one small hand fisted on his chest. Sawyer continued before she could protest, meeting her frantic gaze and silencing her with a look. "Don't take it to the garage. Bring it here. We can put it in the shed."

Gabe considered that a moment, then shook his head. "I hope you know what the hell you're doing."

Slowly, the woman looked away, hiding her face against him again. Sawyer went up the porch steps to the house. To himself, because he didn't want to alarm anyone else, he muttered, "I hope so, too. But I have my doubts."

2

IF SHE HAD her choice, Honey Malone would have
stayed buried next to the warm, musky male throat
and hidden for as long as possible. For the first time in
over a week, she felt marginally safe, and she was in no
hurry to face reality again, not when reality meant vil-
lains and threats, along with an aching head and a
weakness that seemed to have invaded every muscle in
her body. In varying degrees, she felt dizzy and her
head throbbed. Every other minute, her stomach
roiled. She couldn't even think of food without having
to suppress the urge to vomit. And she was so terribly
cold, from the inside out.

At the moment, she wanted nothing more than to
close her eyes and sleep for a good long time.

But of course, she couldn't.

It was beyond unfair that she'd get sick now, but she
couldn't lie to herself any longer. She *was* sick, and it
was sheer dumb luck that she hadn't killed herself, or
someone else, in the wreck.

She still didn't know if she could trust him. At first,
he'd called her honey, and she thought he knew her
name, thought he might be one of them. But he denied
it so convincingly, it was possible she'd misunder-
stood. He'd certainly made no overt threat to her so far.
All she knew for sure was that he was strong and

warm and he said he only wanted to help her. While he held her, she couldn't find the wit to object.

But then his strong arms flexed, and she found herself lowered to a soft bed. Her eyes flew open wide and she stared upward at him—until her head began to spin again. "Oh, God." She dropped back, trying to still the spinning of the room.

"Just rest a second."

More cautiously now, she peeked her eyes open. The man—Sawyer, he said his name was—picked up a white T-shirt thrown over the footboard and pulled it on. It fit him snugly, molding to his shoulders and chest. He wasn't muscle-bound, but rather leanly cut, like an athlete. His wide solid shoulders tapered into a narrow waist. Faded jeans hugged his thighs and molded to his...

Face flaming, she looked down at the soft mattress he'd put her on. Her drenched, muddy jeans were making a mess of things. "The quilt—"

"Is an old one. Don't worry about it. A little lake water isn't going to hurt anything." So saying, he pulled another quilt from the bottom of the bed and folded it around her chest, helping to warm her. She gratefully snuggled into it.

That taken care of, he looked over his broad shoulder to the door, and as if he'd commanded it, his son appeared, carrying a medical bag. Casey looked nonplussed to see where his father had put her. "Ah, Dad, I already got a bed ready for her, the one in the front room."

Sawyer took the medical bag from Casey, then said, "This one will do."

"But where will you sleep?"

On alert, Honey listened to the byplay between father and son. Casey was earnest, she could see that much in his young, handsome face, but Sawyer had his back to her so she could only guess at his expression.

"Casey, you can go help Gabe, now."

"But—"

"Go on."

Casey reluctantly nodded, casting a few quick glances at Honey. "All right. But if you need anything else—"

"If I do, I'll holler."

The boy went out and shut the door behind him. Nervously, Honey took in her surroundings. The room was gorgeous, like something out of a *Home Show* magazine. She'd never seen anything like it, and for the moment, she was distracted. Pine boards polished to a golden glow covered the floor, three walls and the ceiling. The furnishings were all rustic, but obviously high quality. Black-and-white checked gingham curtains were at the windows that took up one entire wall, accompanied by French doors leading out the back to a small patio. The wall of glass gave an incredible view of the lake well beyond.

There was a tall pine armoire, a dresser with a huge, curving mirror, and two padded, natural wicker chairs. In one corner rested a pair of snow skis and a tennis racket, in the other, several fishing poles. Assorted pieces of clothing—a dress shirt and tie, a suit jacket, a pair of jeans—were draped over bedposts and chair backs. The polished dresser top was laden with a few bills and change, a small bottle of aftershave, some crumpled receipts and other papers, including an open book. It was a tidy room, but not immaculate by any measure.

And it was most definitely inhabited by a man. *Sawyer*. She gulped.

Summoning up some logic in what appeared a totally illogical situation, she asked, "What will your wife—"

"I don't have a wife."

"Oh." She didn't quite know what to think about that, considering he had a teenage son, but it wasn't her place to ask, and she was too frazzled to worry about it, anyway.

"Your clothes are going to have to come off, you know."

Stunned by his unreserved statement, she thought about laughing at the absurdity of it; that, or she could try to hide.

She was unable to work up enough strength for either. Her gaze met his. He stared back, and what she saw made her too warm, and entirely too aware of him as a man, even given the fact she was likely in *his* bedroom and at his mercy. She should have been afraid; she'd gotten well used to that emotion. But strangely, she wasn't. "I—"

The door opened and a man stepped in. This one looked different than both Sawyer and the younger man, Gabe. Sawyer had dark, coal black hair, with piercing eyes almost the same color. His lashes were sinfully long and thick and, she couldn't help noticing, he had a lot of body hair. Not too much, but enough that she'd taken notice. Of course, she'd spent several minutes pressed to that wide chest, so it would have been pretty difficult *not* to notice. And he'd smelled too good for description, a unique, heady scent of clean, male sweat and sun-warmed flesh and something more, something that had pervaded her muscles as surely as the weakness had.

Gabe, the one now fetching items from her car, was blond-haired and incredibly handsome. In his cutoffs, bare feet and bare chest, he'd reminded her of a beach bum.

His eyes, a pale blue, should have looked cool, but instead had seemed heated from within, and she'd naturally drawn back from him. His overwhelming masculinity made her uneasy, whereas Sawyer's calm, controlled brand of machismo offered comfort and patience and rock steady security, which she couldn't help but respond to as a woman. Accepting his help felt right, but the very idea alarmed her, too. She couldn't involve anyone else in her problems.

Now this man, with his light brown hair and warm green eyes, exuded gentle curiosity and tempered strength. Every bit as handsome as the blond one, but in a more understated way, he seemed less of a threat. He looked at her, then to Sawyer. "Casey says we have a guest?"

"She ran her car into the lake. Gabe and Casey are off taking care of that now, getting as much of her stuff out of it as they can."

"Her stuff?"

"Seems she was packed up and moving." He flicked a glance at Honey, one brow raised. She ignored his silent question.

"Care to introduce me?"

Sawyer shrugged. He gestured toward her after he took a stethoscope out of his bag. "Honey, this is my brother Jordan."

Jordan smiled at her. And he waited. Sawyer, too, watched her, and Honey was caught. He'd called her by name again, so why did he now look as if he was waiting for her to introduce herself? She firmed her mouth. After a second, Jordan frowned, then skirted a worried look at his brother. "Is she...?"

Sawyer sighed. "She can talk, but she's not feeling well. Let's give her a little time."

Jordan nodded briskly, all understanding and sympathy. Then he looked down at the floor and smiled. "Well, hello there, honey. You shouldn't be in here."

Honey jumped, hearing her name again, but Jordan wasn't speaking to her. He lifted a small calico cat into his arms, and she saw the animal had a bandaged tail. As Jordan stroked the pet, crooning to her in a soothing tone, the cat began a loud, ecstatic purring. Jordan's voice was rough velvet, sexy and low, and Honey felt almost mesmerized by it. It was the voice of a seducer.

Good grief, she thought, still staring. Was every man in this family overflowing with raw sexuality?

"A new addition," Jordan explained. "I found the poor thing on my office doorstep this morning."

Rolling his eyes, Sawyer said to Honey, "My brother is a vet—and a sucker for every stray or injured animal that crosses his path."

Jordan merely slanted a very pointed look at Honey and then said to Sawyer, "And you're any different, I suppose?"

They both smiled—while Honey bristled. She didn't exactly take to the idea of being likened to a stray cat.

"Jordan, why don't you put the cat in the other room and fetch some tea for our guest? She's still chilled, and from the sounds of her cough, her throat is sore."

"Sure, no problem."

But before he could go, another man entered, and Honey could do no more than stare. This man was the biggest of the lot, a little taller than even Sawyer and definitely more muscle-bound. He had bulging shoulders and a massive chest and thick thighs. Like Sawyer, he had black hair, though his was quite a bit longer and somewhat unruly. And his eyes were blue, not the pale blue of Gabe's, but dark blue, almost like her own but more piercing, more intent. She saw no softness, no giving in his gaze, only ruthlessness.

He had a noticeable five o'clock shadow, and a stern expression that made her shiver and sink a little deeper into the bed.

Sawyer immediately stepped over to her and placed his hand on her shoulder, letting her know it was okay, offering that silent comfort again. But she still felt floored when he said, "My brother Morgan, the town sheriff."

Oh, God. A *sheriff*? How many damn brothers did this man have?

"Ignore his glare, honey. We pulled him from some unfinished business, no doubt, and he's a tad... disgruntled."

Jordan laughed. "Unfinished business? That wouldn't be female business, would it?"

"Go to hell, Jordan." Then Morgan's gaze landed

heavily on Honey, though he spoke to Sawyer. "Gabe called me. You mind telling me what's going on?"

Honey was getting tired of hearing Sawyer explain. She looked up at him and asked in her rough, almost unrecognizable voice, "Just how many brothers do you have?"

Jordan smiled. "So she does have a voice."

Morgan frowned. "Why would you think she didn't?"

And Sawyer laughed. "She's been quiet, Morgan, that's all. She's sick, a little disoriented and naturally wary of all of you overgrown louts tromping in and out."

Then to Honey, he said, "There's five of us, including my son, Casey. We all live here, and as it seems you're going to stay put for a spell, too, it's fortunate you've already met them all."

His statement was received with varying reactions. She was appalled, because she had no intention at all of staying anywhere. It simply wasn't safe.

Jordan looked concerned. Morgan looked suspicious.

And in walked Gabe, toting a box. "Nearly everything was wet by the time I got there, except this box of photos she had stashed in the back window. I figured it'd be safer in the house. Casey is helping to unload everything else from the truck, but it's all a mess so we're stowing it in the barn for now. And it looks like it might rain soon. It clouded up real quick. I think we're in for a doozy."

Honey glanced toward the wall of windows. Sure enough, the sky was rapidly turning dark and thick, purplish storm clouds drifted into view. Just what she needed.

Sawyer nodded. "Thanks, Gabe. If it starts to lightning, have Casey come in."

"I already told him."

"Morgan, can you get the county towing truck in the morning and pull her car out of the lake? I want to put it in the shed."

Morgan rubbed his rough jaw with a large hand. "The shed? Why not Smitty's garage so it can be fixed? Or do I even want to know?"

"It's a long story, better explained *after* I find out what ails her. Which I can't do until you all get the hell out of here."

The brothers took the hint and reluctantly began inching out. Before they could all go, though, Sawyer asked, "Any dry clothes in her things, Gabe?"

"Nope, no clothes that I saw. Mostly it's books, hair stuff...junk like that." He dropped the box of framed photos on the floor in front of the closet.

"I don't suppose any of you have a housecoat?"

Three snorts supplied his answer.

If Honey hadn't been feeling so wretched, she would have smiled. And she definitely would have explained to Sawyer that the clothes she wore would have to do, because she wasn't about to strip out of them.

"Any type of pajamas?"

He got replies of, "You've got to be kidding," and, "Never use the things," while Morgan merely laughed.

Squeezing her eyes shut, Honey thought, *No, no, they're not all telling me they sleep in the nude!* She did her best not to form any mental images, but she was surrounded by masculine perfection in varying sizes and styles, and a picture of Sawyer resting in this very bed, naked as a Greek statue, popped into her brain. Additional heat swept over her, making her dizzy again. She could almost feel the imprint of his large body, and she trembled in reaction. She decided it was her illness making her muddled; she'd certainly never been so focused on her sexuality before. Now, she was acutely aware of it.

She opened her eyes and would have shaken her head to clear it, but she was afraid the motion would make her unsettled stomach pitch again.

Casey stuck his head into the room. "I have an old baseball jersey that'd fit her."

"No, thank you—"

Sawyer easily overrode her. "Good. Bring it here."

The brothers all looked at each other, grinning, then filed out. Sawyer leaned down close, hands on his hips, and gave her a pointed frown. "Now."

"Now what?" All her worries, all the fears, were starting to swamp back in on her. She coughed, her chest hurting, her head hurting worse. She felt weak and shaky and vulnerable, which automatically made her defensive. "I'll be fine. If...if Morgan would pull my car out, I'd be appreciative. I'll pay you for your trouble...."

Sawyer interrupted, shaking his head and sitting on the side of the bed. "You're not paying me, dammit, and you aren't going anywhere."

"But..."

"Honey, even if he gets your car out in the morning—and there's no guarantee, figuring how it's stuck in the mud and it looks like a storm's on the way—but even if he did, the car will need repairs."

"Then I'll walk."

"Now why would you wanna do that? Especially considering you can barely stand." His tone turned gentle, cajoling. He produced a thermometer and slipped it under her tongue, making it impossible for her to reply. "We have plenty of room here, and you need someone to look after you until you're well."

She pulled out the thermometer. "It's...it's not safe."

"For you?"

Honey debated for a long moment, considering all her options. But he was trying to help, and with every second that passed, she grew more tired. The bed was so soft, the quilt warm, if she was going to move, it had to be now before she got settled and no longer wanted to. She started to sit up, but Sawyer's large, competent hands on her shoulders gently pressed her back on the bed.

Not bothering to hide his exasperation, he said, "Okay, this is how it's going to be. You're either going to tell me what's going on, or I'm going to take you to the hospital. Which'll it be?"

She searched his face, but the stubbornness was there, along with too much determination. She simply wasn't up to fighting him. Not right now.

"It's not safe because..." She licked her lips, considered her words, then whispered, "Someone is trying to hurt me."

Sawyer stared at her, for the moment too stunned to speak.

"Is this something I should know about, Sawyer?" Morgan asked.

He almost groaned. Wishing he could remove the fear from her eyes, he gave her a wink, then turned to face his most difficult brother. "Eavesdropping, Morgan?"

"Actually, I was doing tea duty." He lifted a cup and saucer for verification. "Hearing the girl's confession was just a bonus."

"It wasn't a confession. She's confused from—"

"No." Trembling, she scooted upward on the bed, clutching the quilt to her chest. She chewed her lower lip, not looking at Morgan, but keeping her gaze trained on Sawyer. After a rough bout of coughing, she whispered, "I'm not confused, or making it up."

Sawyer narrowed his eyes, perturbed by the sincerity in her tone and the way she shivered. If anything, she sounded more hoarse, looked more depleted. He needed to get the questions over with so he could medicate her, get her completely dry and let her rest. "Okay, so who would want to hurt you?"

"I don't know."

Morgan set the tea on the bedside table. "*Why* would anyone want to hurt you?"

Tears glistened in her eyes and she blinked furiously. One shoulder lifted, and she made a helpless gesture with her hand. "I..." Her voice broke, and she cleared her throat roughly. Sawyer could tell how much she hated showing her vulnerability. "I don't know."

Agitated, Sawyer shoved Morgan away from where

he loomed over her, then took up his own position sitting next to her on the bed. "Honey—"

The sky seemed to open up with a grand deluge of rain. It washed against the windows with incredible force. Within seconds the sky grew so dark it looked like midnight rather than early evening. Lightning exploded in a blinding flash, followed by a loud crack of thunder that made the house tremble and startled the woman so badly she jumped.

By reflex, Sawyer reached out to her, closing his hand over her shoulder, caressing her, soothing her. "Shh. Everything's okay."

A nervous, embarrassed laugh escaped her. "I'm sorry. I'm not normally so skittish."

"You're sick and you're hurt." Sawyer leveled a look on his brother. "And you aren't going anywhere tonight, so put the thought from your head."

Morgan promptly agreed, but the curling of his lips showed how amused he was by Sawyer's possessive declaration. "Sure thing. We can sort everything out in the morning after you're rested." He slapped Sawyer on the shoulder. "Let the doc here fix you up. You'll feel better in no time."

Casey came in with the baseball jersey. "Sorry, it took me a little while to find it."

Sawyer accepted the shirt. "Good. Now we can get you out of these wet clothes."

Jordan lounged in the doorway, a small half-smile on his mouth. "Need any help?"

And once again, Sawyer had to shove them all out the door. You'd think they'd never seen an attractive woman before, the way they were carrying on, when in

fact they all had more than their fair share of female adoration. But as Sawyer closed the door and turned back
to her, seeing her lounged in *his* bed, her long hair
spread out over *his* pillow, her wide, watchful gaze, he
knew he was acting as out of sorts as the rest of them.
Maybe more so. He'd just never been so damn *aware* of
a woman, yet with this woman, he felt he could already
read her gaze. And he strongly reacted to it.

That just wouldn't do, not if he was going to be her
doctor.

He laid the shirt on the foot of the bed, resolute.
"Come on." After pulling the damp quilt aside, he
hooked his hands beneath her arms, lifted her, then
proceeded to unbutton the shirt he'd loaned her as if he
did such things every day. She was silent for about half
a second before suddenly coming to life. With a gasp,
she began batting at his hands.

"I can do it!" she rasped in her rough, crackly voice.

He cradled her face in his palms. "Are you sure?"

For long seconds they stared at each other, and just
as his heartbeat began to grow heavy, she nodded.

Pulling himself together, Sawyer sighed. "All right."
He suffered equal parts relief and disappointment.
"Get those wet jeans off, and your panties, too. You're
soaked through to the skin and you need to be dry and
warm. Leave your clothes there on the floor and I'll run
them through the wash." He slid open a dresser
drawer and retrieved his own dry jeans and shorts,
then as he was reaching for the door to leave, he added,
"I'll wait right out here. Call me when you're done or if
you need help with anything."

He stepped into the hallway and ran right into every

single one of his brothers. Even his son was there, grinning like a magpie. He glared at them all while he unsnapped and unzipped his wet jeans. They smiled back. "Don't you guys have something to do?"

"Yeah," Gabe said with a wide grin. "We're doing it."

"At times you're entertaining as hell, Sawyer," Jordan added with a chuckle.

Sawyer shucked off his clothes, content to change in the middle of the hallway since they pretty much had him boxed in. He was annoyed as hell, but unwilling to let them all see it. As he stripped down to his skin, Gabe automatically gathered up the discarded clothes, helping without being asked. Then he handed them to Jordan who handed them to Morgan who looked around, saw no one else to give them to and tucked them under his arm.

After he was dressed again, Sawyer crossed his arms over his chest, returning their insolent looks. "And what's that supposed to mean, exactly?"

Morgan snorted. "Only that you're acting like a buck in mating season. You're looming over that poor woman like you think she might disappear at any minute. You're so obvious, you might as well put your brand on her forehead." Morgan pushed away from the wall and ran his hand through his hair. "The problem is, Sawyer, we don't know who she is or what she's hiding."

Sawyer disregarded his brothers' teasing remarks and frowned over their concerns. He didn't need Morgan to tell him there were going to be complications with the woman. His own concern was heavy. "So what do you want me to do? Take her back to her car? Do you want to lock her up for the night until you fit all the pieces together? The woman is sick and needs care before her situation becomes critical."

Casey frowned. "Is she really that bad off, Dad?"

Rubbing his neck, trying to relieve some of the mounting tension, Sawyer said, "I think she has bronchitis, possibly pneumonia. But I haven't exactly had a chance to check her over yet."

Just then every window in the house rattled with a powerful boom of thunder, and in the next second, the lights blinked out. It was dark in the hallway, and all the men started to grumble profanities—until they heard a thump and a short, startled female yelp of pain in the bedroom.

Sawyer reacted first, immediately reaching for the doorknob, then halting when he realized all his brothers intended to follow him in. One by one they plowed into him, crushing him against the door, muttering curses. Over his shoulder, Sawyer barked, "Wait here, dammit!" then hurried in, slamming the door in their curious faces.

The wall of windows in his room offered some light from the almost constant strobe of lightning, but not enough. He searched through the shadows until he located her, sitting on the floor by the bed. Her wide eyes glimmered in the darkness, appearing stunned.

But it was nothing compared to how Sawyer felt when he realized her damp jeans and silky panties were around her ankles—and her upper body was completely bare.

The breath froze in his lungs for a heartbeat, every

muscle in his body clenching in masculine appreciation of the sweet, utterly vulnerable female sight she presented. Lightning flickered, illuminating her smooth, straight shoulders, her full round breasts. Her taut nipples. Her fair hair left silky trails down her body, flowing sensuously over and around her breasts. He felt the stirrings of a desire so deep it was nearly painful, and struggled to suppress his groan of instant need.

Then, with a small sound, she dropped her head forward in defeat and covered her face with her hands. That was all it took to shake him out of his sensual stupor. Determined, he started forward, dredging up full doctor mode while burying his instinctive, basic urges.

But one fact rang loud and clear in his head.

Damn, he was in deep—and he didn't even know her name.

3

SHE WANTED TO DIE. To just curl up and give up and not
have to worry about another thing. She felt beyond
wretched, more embarrassed than she'd ever been in
her life, getting more so with every second that passed,
and she was so tired of worrying, of finding herself in
impossible situations, giving up seemed the best option. She was just so damn weak, she couldn't do anything.

So instead, she got obnoxious. Without raising her
head, she asked, "Are you done gawking?" Her voice
was a hideous thin croak, a mixture of illness, embarrassment and pain. It was all she could do to keep herself sitting upright.

"I'm sorry." He crouched down and lifted her as if
she weighed no more than the damn cat Jordan had
been petting. Very gently, he placed her on the edge of
the bed, then matter-of-factly skimmed her jeans and
underwear the rest of the way off, leaving her totally
bare. In the next instant, he tugged the jersey over her
head. He treated her with all the attention and familiarity he might have given a small child, even smoothing down her hair. "There. That's got to be more comfortable."

His voice sounded almost as harsh as her own; she
couldn't quite return his smile.

After pulling back the covers, he raised her legs onto the mattress, pressed her back against the headboard with a pillow behind her, then said, "Wait right here while I get some light."

He was gone only a moment, but from the time he stepped out into the hallway until he returned, she heard the drone of masculine voices, some amused, some concerned, some insistent.

God, what must they think of her? She was an intruder, a pathetic charity case, and she hated it.

Sawyer returned with an old-fashioned glass and brass lantern, a flashlight and a small plastic tote of medicine bottles. He closed the door behind him, shutting out the brothers' curious gazes. For that, at least, she was thankful.

"Now, back to business." He unloaded his arms next to the bed on the nightstand, turning up the lantern so that the soft glow of light spread out, leaving heavy shadows in all the corners of the room. "The town is so small, we lose electricity with nearly every storm. It's not something we get too excited over. By morning the lights will be on."

Morning?

He shook the thermometer, and again stuck it in her mouth. "Leave it there this time."

Oh, boy. He was done with stalling, now operating in total efficiency status. Well, fine. She didn't want to talk to him away. Talking took energy, which she didn't have, and hurt her raw throat and made her stomach jumpier than it already was. She honestly didn't know how much longer she could stay awake. Lethargy pulled at her, making her numb.

He approached again, sitting beside her on the bed. He was so warm, heat seemed to pour off him. He gave her a stern look. "I'm going to listen to your lungs. Just breathe normally through your nose, okay?"

She nodded, and he opened the neckline of the jersey and slipped his hand beneath. He didn't look at her, staring at the far wall instead as if in deep concentration. But his wrist was hot, a burning touch against her sensitive skin, contrasting sharply with the icy coldness of the stethoscope.

She forgot to breathe, forgot everything but looking at his profile, at his too long, too thick lashes, his straight nose, his dark hair falling over his brow in appealing disarray. The lantern light lent a halo to that dark hair and turned his skin into burnished bronze. His jaw was firm, his mouth sexy—

"Normal breaths, honey."

Oh, yeah. She sucked in a lungful of air, accidentally filling her head with his delicious scent. She immediately suffered a coughing fit. Sawyer quickly retrieved the thermometer and looked at it with the flashlight. "Almost a hundred and two." He frowned. "Can you sit forward just a second?"

Without waiting for her reply, he leaned her forward, propping her with his body, practically holding her in an embrace against that wide, strong chest. His arms were long and muscled, his body hard and so wonderfully warm. She wanted to snuggle into him but forced herself to hold perfectly still.

Again, he seemed oblivious to the intimacy of the situation.

She was far, far from oblivious.

He lifted the jersey to listen to her lungs through her back. Honey merely closed her eyes, too mortified to do much else. After a long moment, he made a sound of satisfaction.

He carefully leaned her back and recovered her with the quilt. "You've definitely got bronchitis, and if you'd gone on another day or two, you'd have likely ended up with pneumonia. On top of that, I'd be willing to bet you have a concussion." He gently touched a bruised spot on her forehead with one finger. "You hit the steering wheel hard when the car dove into the lake. I suppose I can only be grateful you were wearing your seat belt."

He sounded a bit censuring, but she nodded, so exhausted she no longer cared.

"Are you allergic to any medications?"

"No."

"Can you swallow a pill okay?"

Again she nodded, words too difficult.

He started to say something else, then looked at her face and hesitated. He sighed. "Honey, I know this is hard for you. Being in a strange house with all these strange men wandering about, but—"

"Your brothers are a bit overwhelming," she rasped in her thick voice, "but I wouldn't exactly call them strange."

He smiled. "Well, I would." He raised his voice and shouted toward the door, "I'd call them strange and obnoxious and overbearing and *rude!*"

Honey heard one of the brothers—she thought it was Gabe—shout back, "I know a lot of women who'd object to the obnoxious part!" and a hum of low masculine laughter followed.

Sawyer chuckled. "They mean well. But like me, they're concerned."

He patted her knee beneath the quilt, then handed her the tea. "You can swallow your pills with this. It's barely warm now."

Honey frowned at the palm full of pills he produced. After all, she didn't really know him, and yet she was supposed to trust him. Even knowing she had no choice, she still hesitated.

Patiently, he explained, "Antibiotics and something for the pain. You'll also need to swallow some cough medicine."

"Wonderful." She threw all the pills down in one gulp, then swallowed almost the entire cup of tea, leaving just enough to chase away the nasty taste of the cough liquid he insisted she take next. Whoever had made the tea went heavy on the sugar—which suited her just fine.

Sawyer took the cup from her and set it aside, then eyed her closely. "The door next to the closet is a half bath. Do you need to go?"

Why didn't she simply expire of embarrassment? She was certainly due. "No," she croaked, then thought to add, "thank you."

He didn't look as if he quite believed her, but was reluctant to force the issue. "Well, if you do, just let me know so I can help you. I don't want you to get up and fall again."

Yeah, right. Not in this lifetime. That was definitely a

chore she would handle on her own—or die trying. "I'm fine, really. I'm just so tired."

Sawyer stood and began pulling the quilts off her. They were damp, so she didn't protest, but almost immediately she began to shiver. Seconds later he recovered her with fresh blankets from the closet. He laid two of them over her, tucking her in until she felt so cozy her body nearly shut down.

"Go on to sleep. I'll come back in a couple of hours to check on you—because of the concussion," he added, when she blinked up at him. "I'm sorry, honey, but I'll have to wake you every hour or two just to make certain you're okay. All you'll have to do is open those big blue eyes and say hi, all right?"

"All right." She didn't really like the idea, because she knew she wouldn't be able to sleep a wink now, worrying about when he'd come in, if she'd be snoring, if she'd even make sense. Usually she slept like the dead, and very little could disturb her, but since this had started she'd been so worried, and she'd had to be on her guard at all times.

At least now she could rest in peace and quiet for a while, and that was more than she'd had recently.

Sawyer tucked a curl of hair behind her ear and smoothed his big thumb over her cheek. The spontaneous, casual touches disconcerted her. They weren't what she was used to and she didn't quite know what to think of them. He acted as if it were the most natural thing in the world for him to pet her, which probably meant it was merely his way and had no intimate connotations attached. He was, after all, a doctor.

Still, his touch felt very intimate to Honey. Like a lover's caress.

"Holler if you need anything," he said gently. "The family room is close enough so one of us will hear you."

He moved the lantern to the dresser top and turned it down very low, leaving just enough light so she wouldn't wake disoriented in the strange room. Outside, the storm still raged with brilliant bursts of light and loud rumbling thunder.

He picked up the flashlight and damp quilts and went out, leaving the door open a crack. Honey rolled slowly to her side and stacked her hands beneath her cheek. His bed was so comfortable, the blankets so soft and cozy. And it smelled like him, all masculine and rich and sexy. Her eyes drifted shut, and she sighed. Sleep would be wonderful, but she really didn't dare. As soon as the storm let up, she had to think about what to do.

Sawyer was a nice man. His whole family was nice; she couldn't put them at risk, couldn't take advantage of their generosity and their trusting nature. She supposed she could call a cab to take her into town and buy another used car there. The one she'd been driving didn't have much value anyway, hardly worth repairing.

But her stuff. They'd unloaded everything into the barn, Gabe said. She hadn't even noticed a barn, and if she found it, could she retrieve everything without alerting them to her intentions? She had no doubt they'd feel honor bound to detain her, thanks to her illness.

She just didn't know what to do. Since she knew she wouldn't be able to sleep, she figured she had plenty of time to come up with a plan.

TWENTY MINUTES LATER Sawyer peeked in on her— again. He couldn't quite seem to pull his gaze away for more than a few minutes, and his thoughts wouldn't budge from her at all. She was in his bed—and he knew it, on every level imaginable.

It had taken her less than two minutes to fall deeply asleep, and since then, he'd been checking her every few minutes, drawn by the sight of her cuddled so naturally, so trustingly in his bed. He leaned in the door frame, watching her sleep, enthralled by the way the gentle lantern light played over the curves and hollows of her body.

"She doin' okay?"

Sawyer quickly pulled the door shut as he turned to face Jordan. "She's asleep, and her breathing sounds just a little easier. But she's still really sick. I think she needs some rest more than anything else. She's plain wore out."

"If you want, we can all spell you a turn on waking her up through the night."

"No."

Jordan's eyes narrowed. "Sawyer, it's dumb for you to do it alone. We could—"

"I'm the doctor, Jordan, so I'll do it." He was determined to get his brother's mind off altruistic motives and away from the room. "The rest of you don't need to worry. It's under control."

Jordan studied him a long minute before finally

shrugging. "Suit yourself. But I swear, you're acting damn strange."

Sawyer didn't refute that. His behavior did seem odd, considering his brother didn't know why he was so insistent. But when Jordan walked away, Sawyer again opened the door where she slept. Nope, he didn't want his brothers seeing her like this.

The little lady slept on her stomach, and she kept kicking her covers off; the jersey had ridden to her waist.

Damn, but she had a nice backside. Soft, white, perfectly rounded. The kind of backside that would fit a man's hands just right. His palms tingled at the thought, and his fingers flexed the tiniest bit.

With a small appreciative smile, Sawyer once again covered her. At least her fever must be lower, or she'd still be chilled deep inside. The fact she felt comfortable enough not to need the blankets proved the medicine was doing its job. Still, he touched her forehead, smoothed her hair away, then forced himself to leave the room.

When he walked out this time he ran into Morgan. "We need to talk."

Sawyer eyed his brother's dark countenance. He'd have been worried, except Morgan pretty much always looked that way. "If you're going to offer your help, don't bother. I'm more than able to—"

"Nope. I figure if you want to hover all night over the little darling, that's your business. But I want to show you something."

For the first time, Sawyer noticed Morgan was gripping a woman's purse in his fist. "Our guest's?"

"Yep. I decided I didn't like all this secretive business, and being she's staying here, I was fully justified—"

"You snooped, didn't you?"

Morgan tried to look affronted and failed. "Just took a peek at her wallet for I.D. I'm a sheriff, and I had just cause with all this talk of someone hunting her and such."

"And?" Sawyer had to admit to his own overwhelming curiosity. He wondered if the name would match the woman. "Don't keep me in suspense."

"You won't believe this, but it's *Honey Malone*." Morgan chuckled. "Damn, she sounds just like a female mobster, doesn't she?"

It took Sawyer two seconds before he burst out laughing. *Honey*. No wonder she thought he knew her name. He was still grinning when Morgan poked him.

"It's not that funny."

"Ah, but it is! Especially when you know the joke."

"But you're not going to share it?"

Sawyer shook his head. "Nope. At least, not until I've shared it with Miss Malone."

Since he had the arrogant habit of refusing ever to let anyone rile him, Morgan merely shrugged. "Suit yourself. But you should also know I braved this hellish rain to run out to the car radio and run a check on her. Nothing, from either side of the law. No priors, no complaints, no signed statements. If someone is trying to hurt her, the police don't know a damn thing about it."

Sawyer worked that thought over in his mind, then shook his head. "That could mean several things."

"Yeah, like she's making it all up." Morgan hesitated, but as he turned to walk away, he added, "Or she's more rattled than you first thought and is delusional. But either way, Sawyer, be on your guard, okay?"

"I'm not an idiot."

"No." Morgan pointed at him and chuckled. "But you are acting like a man out to stake a claim. Don't let your gonads overrule your common sense."

Sawyer glared, but Morgan hadn't waited around to see it. Ridiculous. So he was attracted to her, so what? He was human, and he'd been attracted to plenty of women in his day. Not quite this attracted, not quite this...*consumed*. But it didn't matter. He had no intentions of getting involved any more than necessary to get her well. She was a patient, and he'd treat her as such. Period.

But even as he thought it, he opened the door again, drawn by some inexplicable need to be near her.

Damn, but she looked sweet resting there in his bed. Incredibly sweet and vulnerable.

And once again, she'd kicked the blanket away.

HONEY WOKE slowly and struggled to orient herself to the sensation of being in strange surroundings. Carefully, she queried her senses, aware of birds chirping in near rapture, the steady drone of water dripping outside and a soft snore. Yet she was awake.

Her throat felt terrible, and she swallowed with difficulty, then managed to get her heavy eyes to open a tiny bit. As soon as she did, she closed them again against a sharp pain in her head. She held her breath until the pain ebbed, easing away in small degrees.

Her body felt weighted down, warm and leaden, and a buzzing filled her head. It took a lot of effort to gather her wits and recall where she was and why.

She was on her stomach, a normal position for her, and this time she opened her eyes more carefully, only a slit, and let them adjust to the dim light filtering into the room. As her eyes focused on the edge of a blanket, pulled to her chin, she shifted, but her legs didn't want to move. Confused, she peered cautiously around the room. The rain, only a light drizzle now, left glittering tracks along the wall of windows, blurring the image of the lake beyond and the fog rising from it. The gutters must have been overloaded because they dripped steadily, the sound offering a lulling, soporific effect. The day was gray, but it was definitely morning, and the birds seemed to be wallowing in the freshness of it, singing their little hearts out.

Frowning, she looked away from the windows, and her gaze passed over Sawyer, then snapped back. She almost gasped at the numbing pain that quick eye movement caused.

Then she did moan as the sight of him registered.

Wearing nothing more than unsnapped jeans, he lounged in a padded wicker chair pulled close at an angle to the foot of the bed. His long legs were stretched out, his bare feet propped on the edge of the mattress near her waist pinning her blankets in place. No wonder her legs didn't want to move. They couldn't, not with his big feet keeping her blankets taut.

She remembered him waking her several times

throughout the night, his touch gentle, his voice low and husky as he insistently coaxed her to respond to him, to answer his questions. Her skin warmed with the memory of his large hands on her body, smoothing over her, resettling her blankets, lifting her so she could take a drink or swallow another pill.

She warmed even more as she allowed her eyes to drink in the sight of him. Oh, she was awake now. Wide awake. Sawyer had that effect on her, especially when he was more naked than not, available to her scrutiny. He was a strong man, confident, even arrogant in his abilities. But there was an innate gentleness in his touch, and an unwavering serenity in his dark eyes.

The muscles of his chest and shoulders were exaggerated by the long shadows. She felt cool in the rainy, predawn morning, yet he looked warm and comfortable in nothing more than his jeans. His abdomen, hard and flat, had a very enticing line of downy black hair bisecting it, dipping into those low-fitting jeans. Her heart rate accelerated, her fingers instinctively curling into the sheets as she thought about touching him there, feeling how soft that hair might be and how hard the muscles beneath it were.

One of his elbows was propped on the arm of the chair, offering a fist as a headrest. His other arm dangled off the side of the chair, his hand open, his fingers slack. He was deeply asleep, and even in his relaxed state his body looked hard and lean and too virile for a sane woman to ignore. He appeared exhausted, and no wonder after caring for her all night. She studied his whisker-roughened face a moment, then gave in to temptation and visually explored his body again. A soft sigh escaped her.

She needed a drink. She needed the bathroom. But she could be happy just lying there looking at him for a long, long time.

"G'mornin'."

With a guilty start, her attention darted back to his face. His eyes were heavy-lidded, his thick black lashes at half-mast, his dark gaze glittering at her. Honey closed her own eyes for a moment, trying to get her bearings. His voice had been low, sleepy, *sexy*.

Ahem. "Good morning." The words, which she'd meant to be crisp, sounded like a faint, rusty impersonation.

Sawyer tilted his head. "Throat still sore?"

She nodded, peeking a glance at him and quickly looking away again. "You're, ah, pinning my blankets down."

She heard the amusement in his tone when he murmured, "Yeah, I know."

Then he dragged his feet off the bed and stood and stretched—right there in front of her, putting on an impressive display of flexing muscle and sinew and masculine perfection. Without even thinking about it, she rolled to her back to watch him, keeping her blankets high.

With one arm over his head, she saw the dark silky hair beneath his arm, the way his biceps bulged, and she heard his growled rumble of pleasure. As he stretched, his abdomen pulled tighter and the waistband of his jeans curled away from his body. Her vision blurred. He ran both hands through his hair and over his face, then he smiled.

She tried to smile back, she really did. But then he scratched his belly, drawing her gaze there, and she saw that his jeans rode even lower on his slim hips and that his masculine perfection had changed just a tad. Okay, more than a tad. A whole lot more.

He had an erection.

She didn't exactly mean to stare, but since he was standing only a foot away from the bed and she was lying down and he was so close, it was rather hard to ignore. Heat bloomed in her belly, making her toes curl.

He reached out and placed a warm palm on her forehead. "Your fever seems to be down. Luckily, the electricity came on in the middle of the night, otherwise, without the air-conditioning, the house would have been muggy as hell. If this rain ever stops, they're predicting a real scorcher, and with you being sick I'd hate for you to suffer through the heat, too." He smoothed her hair away from her set face, looking at her closely. "You want to use the john?"

She was so flustered by his good-natured chatter in light of her lascivious thoughts, she couldn't answer, even though her situation was beginning to get critical.

He solved the problem for her. Whisking the covers aside, he hooked one arm behind her and levered her upright. She scrambled to get the jersey shirt pulled down over her hips, covering her decently. He didn't seem to notice her predicament.

"Come on. I'll help you in, then wait out here."

She didn't want him waiting anywhere, but he hustled her out of the bed and toward the bathroom, holding her closely, not really giving her time to think about it. He walked her right up to the toilet, then cautiously let her go. "If you need anything, don't be too squeamish to call out, okay?"

Never, not in a million years. She stared at him, blinked twice, then nodded, just to get him out of the room. With a smile and a touch to her cheek, he backed out and pulled the door shut.

Even in her dazed state, Honey was able to appreciate the incredibly beautiful design of the bathroom. Done in the same polished pine but edged with black ceramic tile, it looked warm and masculine and cozy. The countertops were white with black trim, and there was a shower stall but no tub, a black sink, and a small blocked window with the same black-checked gingham curtains. Amazing that a household of men would have such a nice, clean, well-designed home.

After she'd taken care of business, Honey washed her hands, splashed her face and took a long drink of water. She looked at herself in the round etched mirror over the sink and nearly screamed. She looked horrid. Her hair was tangled, her face pale, the bruise on her forehead providing her only color, and that in shades of gray and purple and green. God, she looked as sickly as she felt, and that was saying a lot!

She glanced longingly at the shower, but then she heard Sawyer ask impatiently, "Everything okay?"

It would take more time and effort than she could muster to make herself look any better. With a sigh, she edged her way to the door, holding on to the sink for support. She barely had the door open and he was there, tall, shirtless, overwhelmingly potent. Without a word he wrapped his arm around her and practically carried her back to the bed.

He tucked her in, then asked, "Would you like some tea or coffee?"

Her mouth watered. Now that she wasn't so tired, she noticed other needs, and hot coffee sounded like just the thing to clear out the cobwebs and relieve her sore throat. "I'd kill for coffee."

"When you don't have the strength to swat a fly? Never mind. Nothing so drastic is necessary. The coffee is already on. Morgan and Gabe are both early risers, so one of them has already seen to it because I smell it. Cream and sugar?"

"Please."

He started to turn away, and she said, "Sawyer?"

He looked at her over his shoulder. "Hmm?"

"My things..."

"They're safe. Gabe and Casey got everything stored in the barn before the worst of the storm hit, but if you like, I'll check on them after I've dressed."

After he'd dressed. The fact of his partial nudity flustered her again, and she felt herself blush. She'd simply never been treated to the likes of a man like him before. Her experiences were with more...subtle men. Sawyer without his shirt was more enticing, more overpowering, than most men would have been buck naked.

She cleared her sore throat. "I'd really like my toothbrush. And...and I'd dearly love to shower and get the lake water off—"

"I dunno." He gave her a skeptical look and frowned. "Let's see how you do after eating a little, okay? I don't want you to push it. You still sound like a bullfrog, and I'm willing to bet you have a bit of a fever yet. But first things first. Let me get the coffee. It'll make your throat feel better."

His peremptory manner set her on edge. Straightening her shoulders as much as she could while lying huddled beneath a layer of blankets, she groused, "It's not up to you to decide what I can or can't do."

He halted in mid stride and slowly turned to face her. The intensity of his dark gaze almost made her squirm, but after a good night's rest, she felt emotionally stronger, if not physically, and she couldn't continue to let him baby her or dictate to her. Now was as good a time as any to assert herself.

Tilting his head, he said, "Actually—I can."

"No—"

He stalked forward, startling her with the suddenness of it. His bare feet didn't make a sound on the polished flooring, but he might have been stomping for the expression on his face. Bracing one hand on the headboard and the other on the pillow by her cheek, he leaned down until their noses almost touched. Her head pressed into the pillow, but there was no place to retreat to, no way to pull back.

His breath touched her as he studied her face. "You're seriously ill, and I didn't stay up all night checking on you just so you could turn stubborn this morning and set yourself on a decline."

She mustered her courage and frowned up at him. "I know I'm not a hundred percent well, but—"

He made a rude sound to that statement. "It's a wonder you even made it to the bathroom on your own. I can tell just looking at your flushed cheeks and lips that you still have a fever. What you need is plenty of rest and medicine and liquids."

She hated to sound vain, so the words came out in a rough, embarrassed whisper. "I smell like the lake."

At first his brows lowered and he stared at her. Then, almost against his will it seemed, he leaned closer and his nose nearly touched her throat beneath her ear. She sucked in a startled breath, frozen by his nearness, his heat, the sound of his breathing. He nuzzled gently for just a moment, then slowly leaned away again, and his gaze traveled down her throat to her chest and beyond, then came back to her face, and there was a new alertness to his expression, a sensual hardness to his features.

She swallowed roughly and croaked, "Well?" trying to hide the effect he'd had on her, trying, and failing, to be as cavalier.

His lips twitched, though his eyes still looked hot and far too intent. He touched her cheek, then let his hand fall away. "Not a single scent of lake, I promise. Quit worrying about it."

She couldn't quit worrying, not when he stayed so close. And she knew a shower would revive her spirits, which she needed so she could think clearly. She tried a different tack. "I'm not used to going all day without a shower. I'll feel better after I clean up."

He continued to loom over her, watching her face, then finally he sighed. "Somehow I doubt that, but then, what do I know? I'm just the doctor." When she started to object, he added, "If you feel such a strong need to get bathed, fine. I'll help you, and no, don't start shaking your head at me. I'm not leaving you alone to drown yourself."

"You're also not watching me bathe!"

He started to grin, but rubbed his chin quickly instead. "No, of course not. The shower is out because I doubt you could stand that long. And as wobbly as you seem when you're on your feet, I'm not taking the chance. But this afternoon, after I've seen a few patients, I'll take you to the hall bath. We have a big tub you can soak in. By then I'll have your clothes run through the washer, and you can wear your own things. We'll manage, I think."

Worse and worse. "Sawyer, I don't want you doing my laundry."

"There's no one else, Honey. Morgan has to go into the office today, and Jordan is making a few housecalls. Casey has never quite learned the knack of doing laundry, though I'm working on him, and if I know Gabe, he'll be off running around somewhere."

She stared at him, dumbfounded, then shook her head. "Let me clarify. I don't want *any* of you doing my laundry."

"The clothes you came in are wet and muddy. By now, they probably do smell like the lake. Unless you want to continue living in Casey's shirt, someone needs to do it, and you're certainly not up to it." She started to speak, and he held up a hand. "Give over, will you? I doubt doing a little laundry will kill me. If it did, I'd have been dead a long time ago."

She seemed to have no options at all. With a sigh, she said, "Thank you."

"You're welcome."

His continued good humor made her feel like a nag. Trying to get back to a more neutral subject, she asked, "Do you see patients every day?"

He straightened from the bed. "Don't most doctors?"

"I really don't know."

"Well, they do. You can take my word on it. Illness has no respect for weekends or vacations. And since I'm the only doctor around for miles, I've gotten used to it."

Nervously pleating the edge of the blanket, she wondered if this might be her best chance to slip away. It was for certain if he didn't want her up to shower, he wouldn't want her up to leave on her own. "Do you have an office close by?"

He crossed his arms over his chest. "Very close."

"Oh?" She tried to sound only mildly interested.

"You're not going anywhere, Honey."

Her tongue stuck to the roof of her mouth.

"Don't look so shocked. I could see you plotting and planning."

"But...how?" She'd kept her expression carefully hidden. At least, she thought she had.

"I can read you."

"You don't even know me!"

He looked disgruntled by that fact. "Yeah, well, for whatever reason, I know you well enough already to see how your mind works. What'd you think to do? Hitchhike into town when we were all away from the house?"

She hadn't, simply because she hadn't thought that far ahead yet. But it might not have been a bad idea.

She'd be able to tell by the license plates if the driver was local or not, ridding the risk of being picked up by the people who were after her.

When she remained quiet, he shook his head and muttered, "Women." He went out the door without another word, and Honey let him. She had a lot to think about. This might be her only chance to save Sawyer and his family from getting involved. She'd left in the first place to protect her sister. The last thing she wanted to do was get someone else in trouble.

Especially such an incredible man as Sawyer.

4

SAWYER TAPPED on the door and then walked in. Honey was in the bed, her head turned to the window. She seemed very pensive, but she glanced at him as he entered. He saw her face perk up at the sight of the tray he carried.

Grinning, he asked, "So you're hungry?"

She slid higher in the bed. "Actually...yes. What have you got there?"

He set the tray holding the coffee and other dishes on the dresser and carried another to her, opening the small legs on the tray so it fit over her lap. "Gabe had just pulled some cinnamon rolls from the oven, so they're still hot. I thought you might like some."

"Gabe cooks?"

Sawyer handed her the coffee, then watched to make sure it was to her liking. Judging by the look of rapture on her face as she sipped, it was just right. "We all cook. As my mom is fond of saying, she didn't raise no dummies. If a man can't cook, especially in a household devoid of women, he goes hungry."

She'd finished half the cup of coffee right off so he refilled her cup, adding more sugar and cream, then gave her a plate with a roll on it. The icing had oozed over the side of the roll, and she quickly scooped up a fingerful, then moaned in pleasure as she licked her finger clean.

Sawyer stilled, watching her and suffering erotic images that leaped into his tired, overtaxed brain. His reactions to her were getting way out of hand. Of course, they'd been out of hand since he'd first seen her. And last night, when she kept kicking the covers away, he'd almost gone nuts. Pinning them down with his feet had been a form of desperate self-preservation.

He hadn't had such a volatile reaction to a woman in too many years to count. No, he'd never been entirely celibate, but he had always been detached. Now, with this woman who remained more a stranger than otherwise, he already felt far too involved.

He cleared his throat, enthralled by the appreciative way she savored the roll. "Good?"

"Mmm. Very. Give my regards to the chef."

She sounded so sincere, he almost laughed. "It's just a package that you bake. But Gabe really can do some great cooking when he's in the mood. Usually everyone around here grabs a snack first thing in the morning, then around eight they hit Ceily's diner and get breakfast."

"If they can cook, why not eat here?"

He liked it that she was more talkative today, and apparently more at ease. "Well, let's see. Gabe goes to town because that's what he always does. He sort of just hangs out."

Her brows raised. "All the time?"

With a shrug, he admitted, "That's Gabe. He's a handyman extraordinaire—his title, not mine—so he's never without cash. Someone's always calling on him to fix something, and there's really nothing he can't fix." Including her car, though Sawyer hadn't asked him to fix it. Not yet. "He keeps busy when he wants. And when he doesn't, he's at the lake, lolling in the sun like a big fish."

Gabe stuck his head in the door to say, "I resent that. I bask, I do not loll. That makes me sound lazy."

Sawyer saw Honey gulp the bite in her mouth and almost choke as she glanced up at his brother. As a concession to their guest, Gabe had pulled on frayed jean shorts rather than walking around in his underwear. He hoped Jordan and Morgan remembered to do the same. They each had more than enough female companionship, but never overnight at the house, so they were unused to waking with a woman in residence.

Gabe hadn't shaved yet, and though he had on a shirt, it wasn't buttoned so his chest was mostly bare. Sawyer shook his head at his disreputable appearance. "You are lazy, Gabe."

Gabe smiled at Honey. "He's just jealous because he has so much responsibility." Then to Sawyer, "Now, if I was truly lazy, would I plan on fixing the leak in your office sink this morning?"

Sawyer hesitated, pleased, then took a sip of coffee before nodding. "Yeah, you would, considering you can't go to the lake because it's raining."

"Not true. The best fishing is done in the rain."

He couldn't debate that. "Are you really going to fix the sink?"

"Sure. You said it's leaking under the cabinet?"

Sawyer started to explain the exact location of the

leak, but Honey interrupted, asking, "Where is his office?"

Gabe hitched his head toward the end of the hallway. "At the back of the house. He and my dad built it on there after he got his degree and opened up his own practice. 'Course, I helped because Sawyer is downright pathetic with a hammer. He can put in tiny stitches, but he has a hell of a time hitting a nail or cutting a board straight."

Honey carefully set down her last bite of roll. "Your dad?"

"Yep. He's not a military man, like Sawyer's dad was, but he is a pretty good handyman, just not as good as me."

Standing, Sawyer headed toward Gabe, forcing him to back out of the doorway. He could see the questions and the confusion on Honey's face, but it was far too early for him to go into long explanations on his family history. "Go on and let her drink her coffee in peace."

Gabe put on an innocent face, but laughter shone in his eyes. "I wasn't bothering her!"

"You were flirting."

"Not that she noticed." He grinned shamefully. "She was too busy watching you."

That sounded intriguing—not that he intended to dwell on it or to do anything about it. Likely she watched him because he was the one most responsible for her. "I'll be at the office after I've showered and gotten dressed."

"All right. I'll go get my tools together."

Sawyer stepped back into the room and shut the door, then leaned against it. Just as Gabe had mentioned, Honey watched him, her blue eyes wide and wary. He nodded at her unfinished roll. "You done?"

"Oh." She glanced down at the plate as if just remembering it was there. "Yes." She wiped her fingers on the napkin he'd provided and patted her mouth. "Thank you. That was delicious. I hadn't realized I was so hungry."

Eating less than one cinnamon roll qualified as hungry? He grunted. "More coffee?"

"Yes, please."

Her continued formality and good manners tickled him. Here she was, bundled up in his bed, naked except for his son's jersey, and with every other word she said *please.* She still sounded like a rusty nail on concrete, but she didn't look as tense as she had last night. Probably the need for sleep had been more dire than anything else. As he refilled her cup, emptying the carafe, he said, "I have spare toothbrushes in my office. If you'd like, I can give you one. I'd go get yours, but I'm not sure which box it's in."

"I'm not sure, either."

"Okay, then. I'll fetch you one in a bit." He finished his own coffee while leaning on the dresser, looking at her. "Before I start getting ready for my day, you want to tell me who you are?"

She went so still, it alarmed him. He set down his empty cup and folded his arms over his chest. "Well?"

"I think," she muttered, not quite meeting his gaze, "that it'll be simpler all around if I don't involve you."

"You don't trust me?"

"Trust a man I've known one day?"

"Why not? I haven't done anything to hurt you, have I?"

"No. It's not that. It's just...Sawyer, I can't stay here. I don't want to endanger you or your son or your brothers."

That was so ludicrous he laughed. And her lack of trust, regardless of the time limits, unreasonably annoyed him. "So you think one little scrawny woman is better able to defend herself than four men and a strapping fifteen-year-old?"

Her mouth firmed at his sarcasm. "I don't intend to get into a physical battle."

"No? You're going to just keep running from whatever the hell it is you're running from?"

"That's none of your business," she insisted.

His jaw clenched. "Maybe not, but it would sure simplify the hell out of things if you stopped being so secretive."

She pinched the bridge of her nose and squeezed her eyes shut. Sawyer felt like a bully. Just because she'd sat up and eaten a little didn't mean she was up to much more than that. He sighed in disgust—at himself and her—then pushed away from the dresser to remove the tray from her lap.

She glanced at him nervously. "I...I don't mean to make this more difficult."

He kept his back to her, not wanting her to see his frown. "I realize that. But you're going to have to tell me something sooner or later."

A heavy hesitation filled the air. Then he heard her draw in her breath. "No, I don't. My plans don't concern you."

Everything in him fought against the truth of her words. "You landed in my lake."

"And I offered to pay for the damages."

He turned to face her, his muscles tense. "Forget the damn damages. I'm not worried about that."

She looked sad and resolute. "But payment for the damages is all I owe you. I didn't ask to be brought here. I didn't ask for your help."

"You got it anyway." He stalked close again, unable to keep the distance between them. "No respectable man would leave a sick, frightened woman alone in a rainstorm. Especially a woman who was panicked and damn near delusional."

"I wasn't—"

"You slugged my son. You were afraid of me."

She winced again, then worried her bottom lip between her teeth. His heart nearly melted, and that angered him more than anything else. He sat on the edge of the bed and took her hands in his. "Honey, you can trust me. You can trust us." She didn't quite meet his gaze, staring instead at his throat. "The best thing now is to tell me what's going on so I know what to expect."

She looked haunted as her gaze met his, but she also looked strong, and he wasn't surprised when she whispered, "Or I can leave."

They stared at each other, a struggle of wills, and with a soft oath Sawyer stood and paced away. Maybe he was pushing too fast. She needed time to reason things through. He'd wear her down, little by little. And if that didn't work, he'd have Morgan start an investigation—whether she liked it or not.

One thing was certain. He wasn't letting her out of his sight until he knew it was safe.

With his back to her, his hands braced on the dresser, he said, "Not yet."

"You can't keep me here against my will."

"Wanna bet?" He felt like a bastard, but his gut instincts urged him to keep her close regardless of her insistence. "Morgan is the town sheriff, and he heard everything you said. If nothing else, he'd want to keep you around for questioning. I'm willing to give you some time. But until you're ready to explain, you're not going anywhere."

He could feel her staring at his back, feel the heat of her anger. She wasn't nearly so frail as he'd first thought, and she had more gumption than the damn old mule Jordan kept out in the pasture.

Despite the raspiness of her voice, he heard her disdain when she muttered, "And you wanted me to trust you."

His hand fisted on the dresser, but he refused to take the bait. He pulled open a drawer and got out a pair of shorts, saying over his shoulder, "I need to shower and get dressed before patients start showing up. Why don't you just go on back to sleep for a spell? Maybe things'll look a little different this afternoon."

He saw her reflection in the mirror, the way her eyes were already closing, shutting him out. He wanted to say something more, but he couldn't. So instead he walked away, and he closed the door behind him very softly.

SHE SLEPT the better part of the day. After taking more medicine and cleaning up as much as she could using the toothbrush he provided and the masculine-scented soap in the bathroom, she simply konked out. One minute she'd been disgruntled because he was rushing her back to bed, and the next she was sound asleep. Sawyer roused her once to take more ibuprofen and sip more water, but she barely stirred enough to follow his directions. He held her head up with one hand, aware of the silkiness of her heavy hair and the dreamy look in her sleepy eyes. She smiled at him, too groggy to remember her anger.

Fortunately for him, since he couldn't stay by her side, she hadn't kicked off her blankets again. He'd worried about it, and gone back and forth from his office to her room several times during the day, unable to stay away. After Casey had finished up his chores, he promised to stay close in case she called out.

She hadn't had any lunch, and it was now nearing dinnertime. When Sawyer entered the room, he saw his son sitting on the patio through the French doors. He had the small cat with him that Jordan had brought home. Using a string, he enticed the cat to pounce and jump and roll.

This time Honey was on her back, both arms flung over her head. He could see her legs were open beneath the covers. She was sprawled out, taking up as much room as her small body could in the full-size bed. In his experience, most women slept curled up, like a cat, but not Honey. A man would need a king-size bed to accommodate her.

He was still smiling when he stepped outside with Casey. "She been sleeping okay?"

"Like the dead." Casey glanced up at him, then yelped when the cat attacked his ankle. "She looks like someone knocked her out, doesn't she? I've never seen anyone sleep so hard. The cat got loose and jumped up on the bed and before I could catch her, she'd been up one side and down the other, but the woman never so much as moved."

"She's a sound sleeper, and I think she was pretty exhausted, besides. Thanks for keeping a watch on her."

Sawyer saw a movement out of the corner of his eye and turned. Honey was propped up on one elbow, her hair hanging forward around her face, her eyes squinted at the late afternoon sunshine. Most of the day it had continued to drizzle, and now that the sun was out, the day was so humid you could barely draw a deep breath.

Honey looked vaguely confused, so he went in to her. Casey followed with the cat trailing behind.

"Hello, sleepyhead."

She looked around as if reorienting herself. The small cat made an agile leap onto the bed, then settled herself in a semicircle at the end of Honey's feet, tucking her bandaged tail in tight to sleep. Honey stared at the cat as if she'd never seen one before. "What time is it?"

"Five o'clock. You missed lunch, but dinner will be ready soon."

Casey stepped forward to retrieve the new pet, but Honey shook her head. "She's okay there. I don't mind sharing the bed."

Casey smiled at her. They all loved and accepted animals, thanks to Jordan, and it pleased his son that their guest appeared to be of a similar mind. "You want something to drink?"

She thought about that for a moment, then finally nodded. "Yes, please."

Sawyer was amused by her sluggish responses and said, "Make it orange juice, Case."

"Sure thing."

Once Casey was gone, Sawyer studied her. She yawned hugely behind her hand, then apologized.

"I can't believe I slept so long."

He resisted the urge to say, *I told you so*, and stuck to the facts instead. "You've got bronchitis, which can take a lot out of you, not to mention you're just getting over a concussion. Sleep is the best thing for you."

She sat back and tucked the covers around her waist. After a second, she said, "I'm sorry about arguing with you earlier. I know you mean well."

"But you don't trust me?"

She shrugged. "Trust is a hard thing. I'm not generally the best judge of character."

This sounded interesting, so he pulled up a chair and made himself comfortable. "How so?"

She gave him a wary look, but was saved from answering when Casey came back in. He handed her the glass of iced orange juice and a napkin.

"Thank you."

"No problem." He turned to Sawyer. "I'm going to go down and do some more work on the fence."

"Only for about an hour. Dinner will be ready by then."

"All right."

As Casey started out, Honey quickly set her glass aside and lifted a hand. "Casey!"

He turned, his look questioning.

"I noticed your shoulders are getting a little red. Have you been out in the sun much lately?"

"Uh..." He glanced at his father, then back to Honey. "Yeah, I mean, I've been outside, but there's hasn't really been much sun till just a bit ago."

"I know it's none of my business, but you should really put on a shirt or something. Or at least some sunscreen. You don't want to burn."

Sawyer frowned at her, then looked at Casey. Sure enough, there was too much color on his son's wide shoulders and back. Casey looked, too, then grimaced. "I guess it was so cloudy today, I didn't think about it."

She looked prim as she lectured. "You can burn even through the clouds. I guess because I'm so fair, I'm especially conscious of the sun. But I'd hate to see you damage your skin."

Casey stared at her, looking totally dumbfounded. Too much sunshine was probably the last thing the average fifteen-year-old would have on his mind. "I'll, uh...I'll put some sunscreen on. Thanks."

Sawyer added, "And a shirt, Case."

"Yeah, okay." He hurried out before he drew any more attention.

Sawyer looked at Honey. She was smiling, and she looked so sweet, she took his breath away. He didn't like her interference with his son, but since she was right this time, he couldn't very well lecture her on it.

"You have a wonderful son."

He certainly thought so. "Thank you."

"He doesn't really look like you. Does he take after his mother?"

"No."

She looked startled by his abrupt answer, and Sawyer wished he could reach his own ass to kick it. He didn't want her starting in on questions he didn't want to answer, but his attitude, if he didn't temper it, would prompt her to do just that.

"I got your clothes washed. If you're feeling up to a bath, we can get that taken care of before dinner, then you can change." Not that he wanted her trussed up in lots of clothes when she looked so enticing wearing what she had on. But he knew it'd be safer for his peace of mind if she at least had panties on.

Except that he'd already seen the tiny scrap of peach silk she considered underwear, and knowing she wore that might be worse than knowing she was bare, sort of like very sweet icing on a luscious cake.

Luckily he'd done the laundry while no one else was around. He didn't want his brothers envisioning her in the feminine, sexy underwear. But he knew they would have if they'd seen it. He could barely get the thought out of his mind.

"I'm definitely up for a bath. I feel downright grungy."

She looked far from grungy, but he kept that opinion to himself. "We'll use the hall bath. Morgan's room opens into it, but he isn't home yet. I think he's on a date. And Gabe only uses the shower in the basement."

Her eyes widened. "Good grief. How many bathrooms do you have?"

She looked confused again, and he grinned. "As

many as I have brothers, I guess. Little by little we added on as everyone grew up and needed more room."

"It's amazing you all still live together."

He lifted one shoulder in a lazy shrug. "My father left us the house, and my mom moved to Florida after Gabe graduated. Morgan stays here in the main house with me and Case, but he's building his own place on the south end of the property. It should be done by the end of the summer."

"How much property do you have?"

"Around fifty acres. Most of it's unused and heavily treed, just there for privacy, or if any other family decides to build on it. Morgan'll have his own acreage, but still be close enough, which is the way we all like it. Jordan's settled into the garage. He converted it to an apartment when he was around twenty because he's something of a loner, more so than the rest of us, but with his college bills, he couldn't really afford to move completely out on his own. Now he could, of course, since there's even more call for a vet in these parts than there is for a doctor, but he's already settled. And Gabe has the basement, which runs the entire length of the house. He's got it fixed up down there real nice, with his own kitchen and bath and living room, and his own entrance, though he usually just comes through the house unless he's sneaking a girl in."

"He's not allowed to have women over?"

"Not for the night, but that's not really a rule or anything now, just something my mother started back when Gabe was younger and kept trying it." Sawyer grinned, remembering how often he and his brothers used to get in trouble. "Gabe has always attracted women, and sometimes I think he doesn't quite know what to do with them. Dragging one home for my mother to get rid of seemed to be a favorite plan of his."

Honey chuckled, and he could tell by her expression she didn't know he was serious. He grinned, too. She'd get to know Gabe better, then she'd realize the truth.

"Keeping women out is just something that we've all stuck to. Especially with Casey around. He's old enough now not to be influenced, but he was always a nosy kid, so you couldn't do much without him knowing. He has a healthy understanding of sex, but I didn't want him to be cavalier about it."

She pulled her knees up and rested her crossed arms on them. Smiling, she said, "I guess your wife wouldn't have liked it much, either, if a lot of women had been in and out of the house."

Annoyance brought him to his feet, and he paced to the French doors. The topic shouldn't be a touchy one, and usually wasn't. But Honey didn't know all the circumstances, all the background. He said simply, "My wife never lived in this house."

She didn't reply to that, but he knew she now felt awkward when that hadn't been his intention. He glanced over his shoulder, saw her worried gaze and grimaced at his own idiocy. He'd opened a can of worms with that confession, and he didn't know why. He never discussed his ex-wife with anyone except his family, and then only rarely.

"I got divorced while I was still in medical school. In fact, just a month after Casey was born. She was still pretty young and foolish and she wasn't quite up to being a mother. So I took complete custody. My mother and Gabe's father really helped me out with him until I could get through medical school. Actually, everybody helped. Morgan was around nineteen, Jordan fifteen and Gabe twelve. In a lot of ways, Gabe and Casey are like brothers."

She looked fascinated, almost hungry for more information. He walked over to her and sat again. "What about you? You have much family?"

"No." She looked away, then made a face. "There's only my father and my sister. My mother passed away when I was young."

"I'm sorry." He couldn't imagine how he'd have gotten through life without his mother. She was the backbone of the family, the strongest person he knew and the most loving.

Honey shrugged. "It was a long time ago. I'm not very close with my father, but my sister and I are."

"How old's your sister?"

"Twenty-four."

"How old are you?"

She looked at him suspiciously, as if he'd asked for her Social Security number. After a long hesitation, she admitted, "I'm twenty-five."

He whistled. "Must have been rough for your father, two kids so close in age and your mother gone."

She waved that away. "He hired in a lot of help."

"What kind of help?"

"You know, nannies, cooks, tutors, pretty much everything. My father spent a lot of time at work."

"Didn't he do anything with you himself?"

She laughed, but there wasn't much humor in the sound. "Not a lot. Dad wasn't exactly thrilled to have daughters. I think that's what he hated most about Mother dying—she hadn't given him a son yet. He thought about remarrying a lot, but he was so busy with his business, and he worried that someone would divorce him and get part of it. He was a little paranoid that way."

Sawyer looked her over, searching her face, seeing the signs of strain. She'd put up a brave front, but he could see the hurt in her blue eyes and knew there was a lot about her life that hadn't always been satisfactory. "Sounds like a hell of a childhood you had."

Color washed over her cheeks, and she ducked her face. "I didn't mean to complain. We had a lot more than most kids ever do, so it wasn't bad."

Except it didn't sound like she'd had a lot of love or affection or even attention. Sawyer had always appreciated his family, their support, the closeness, but now he realized just how special those things were. They came without strings, without restriction or embarrassment, and were unconditional.

She was still looking bashful over the whole subject, so he decided to let it drop. At least for now. "I guess if you're going to take that bath, we should get on with it or you'll miss dinner. And Jordan really outdid himself tonight for you."

"Now Jordan's cooking?"

He shrugged. "We take turns. Nothing fancy. I told him to make it light since I wasn't sure what you'd feel up to. He's got chicken and noodles in the Crock-Pot, and fresh bread out of the bread machine."

She shook her head. "Amazing. Men who cook."

Laughing, Sawyer reached for her and helped her out of the bed. She clutched at the top blanket, dragging it off the mattress and disturbing the cat, who looked very put out over the whole thing. Honey apologized to the animal, who gave her a dismissive look and recurled herself to sleep.

"You'll have cat hair in the bed."

"I don't mind if you don't. It's your bed."

"You're sleeping in it."

They stared at each other for a taut, electric moment, then Honey looked away. Her hands shook as she busied herself by wrapping the blanket over and around her shoulders. It dragged the ground, even hiding her feet.

He supposed that was best; even though the jersey covered her from shoulders to knees, he didn't want his brothers ogling her—and they would. They were every bit as aware of an attractive woman as Sawyer, and Honey, in his opinion, was certainly more attractive than most. His brothers might not comment on the sexy picture she made with her hair disheveled, her feet bare and her slender body draped in an overlarge male shirt, but they'd notice.

She seemed steadier now, but he kept his right arm around her and held her elbow with his left hand, just in case. She was firmly in his embrace, and he liked it.

To get his mind off lusty thoughts and back on the subject at hand, he asked, "Don't you know any men who cook?"

She sent him an incredulous look. "My father's never even made his own coffee. I doubt he'd know how. And my fiancé took it for granted that cooking was a woman's job."

They'd almost reached the door, and Sawyer stopped dead in his tracks. His heart punched against his ribs; his thighs tightened. Without even realizing it, his hands gripped her hard as he turned her to face him. "You have a fiancé?"

Her eyes widened. The way he held her, practically on her tiptoes, pulled her off balance, and she braced her palms flat against his chest. He saw her pupils dilate as awareness of their positions sank in. "Sawyer..."

Her voice was a whisper, and he barely heard her over the roaring in his ears. He pulled her a little closer still, until her body was flush against his and her heartbeat mingled with his own. "Answer me, dammit. Are you engaged?"

She didn't look frightened by his barbaric manner, which was a good thing since he couldn't seem to get himself in hand. That word *fiancé* was bouncing off his brain with all the subtlety of a bass drum. If she was going to be married soon...

"Not...not anymore."

"What?" He was so rattled, he wasn't at all sure he understood.

"I'm not engaged, not anymore."

Something turbulent and dangerous inside him settled, but in its place was a sudden blast of violent heat, an awareness of how much her answer had mattered to him.

He looked down at her mouth, saw her parted lips tremble, and he went right over the edge. He leaned down until he could feel her warm breath on his mouth, fast and low, and the vibrancy of her expectation, her own awareness.

And then he kissed her.

5

HONEY CLUTCHED at him, straining to make the contact
more complete. Her blanket fell to the floor in a puddle
around her feet. She barely noticed.

She didn't think about what was happening, and she
didn't think about pulling away. Overwhelmed by
pure sensation, by heat and need she'd never experienced before, she wanted only to get closer. She'd
thought the attraction was one-sided, but now, feeling
the faint trembling in Sawyer's hard body, she knew he
was affected, too.

Sawyer's mouth was warm and firm, and he teased,
barely touching her, giving her time to change her
mind, to pull back. Until she groaned.

There was an aching stillness for half a heartbeat,
then his mouth opened on hers, voraciously hungry,
and his hands slid around to her back, holding her so
tightly she could barely breathe. She felt the hot slide of
his tongue and the more brazen press of his swollen
sex against her belly. A delicious sensation of yearning
unfurled inside her, making her thighs tingle and her
toes curl. Her fever was back, hotter than ever.

A knock sounded on the door.

They both jumped apart, Sawyer with a short vicious
curse, Honey with a strained gasp. She almost fell as
her feet tangled in the forgotten blanket, and would

have if Sawyer hadn't reached out and snagged her close again. He stared down into her face, his expression hard, his gaze like glittering ice, then called out, "What?"

The door opened and Jordan stuck his head in. He took one look at them, made a sheepish face and started to pull it shut again.

Sawyer caught the doorknob, keeping the door open. "What is it?"

Honey fumbled for the blanket, wishing she could pull it completely over her head and hide. It was so obvious Jordan knew exactly what he'd interrupted. Yet she'd only known Sawyer a day and a half, less if you counted how much she'd slept.

It didn't matter to her body, and not really to her heart.

"Dinner'll be ready in about ten minutes." Jordan glanced at her, gave a small smile at her fumbling efforts to cover herself and again tried to sidle out.

"Can you make it twenty?" Sawyer asked, apparently not the least uncomfortable, or else hiding it very well. "She was just about to bathe."

Jordan slanted her an appraising look, and Honey wanted to kick Sawyer. She was off balance, both emotionally and physically. That kiss...wow. She'd never known anything like it. How the hell could he stand there and converse so easily when she could barely get the words to register in her fogged brain? And how could he manage to embarrass her like that?

Firmly, but with a distinct edge to her croaking voice, she said, "I don't want you to hold up dinner on my account." She made a shooing motion with her free hand, trying to be nonchalant. "Just go on and eat. Really."

Jordan caught her fluttering hand and grinned. "Nonsense. We can wait. Morgan is running a little late, anyway. He had some trouble in town."

She felt Sawyer shift and tighten his arm around her. "What kind of trouble?"

"Nothing serious. A cow got loose from the Morrises' property and wandered into the churchyard. Traffic was backed up for a mile."

Honey tilted her head, thrilled for a change of topic. "The cow was blocking traffic?"

"No. Everyone just stopped to gawk. Around here, a cow on the loose is big news." Then, with a totally straight face and a deadpan voice, Jordan added, "Luckily, the cow wasn't spooked too badly by all the attention."

Honey bit back her smile.

At that moment, the cat leaped off the bed to twine around Jordan's ankles. Without even looking down, he scooped up the small pet and cuddled her close, encouraging the melodic, rumbling purr. To Honey, he said, "Go on and take your bath. There's no rush."

They stepped into the hallway en masse, two powerful men, an ecstatic cat and a woman wrapped head to toes in a blanket. They nearly collided with Casey, who was liberally caked in mud. He'd removed his shoes so he wasn't tracking anything in, but mud was on his legs clear to his knees. The shirt he'd worn, thanks to her interference—she still didn't know what had come over her—was dirt and sweat stained. He looked more like a man than ever.

Holding up both hands, Casey said, "Don't come too close. The fields are drenched and muddy as hell...uh, heck. And half that mud is on me."

Jordan clapped him on the back. "Well, you'll have to use Gabe's shower, because the little lady wants a bath."

Casey stared at her.

Honey deduced that the phenomenon of having a female bathing in the all-male household warranted nearly as much attention as a cow on the loose.

Her face was getting redder by the second. If she didn't have a fever, she soon would. Never in her life had bathing been such an ordeal, or been noted and discussed by so many males.

The front door slammed, and not long after, Morgan rounded the hall, already stripping his shirt off with frustrated, jerky movements. Powerful, bulky muscles rippled across his broad shoulders and heavy chest as he stamped around the corner of the hall. He had his hands on the button to his tan uniform slacks when he realized he had an audience.

He didn't look the least discomforted at being caught undressing in the middle of the day, in the middle of the house, in front of a crowd.

"Sorry," he grumbled without an ounce of sincerity, and yanked his belt free. "I'm just heading for the shower. It must be ninety out there, and the damn humidity makes it feel like a sauna." He pointed an accusing finger at Jordan. "It was only the thought of a cool shower that kept me from kicking that damn ornery heifer, who no matter what I tried, refused to budge her big spotted butt."

Jordan laughed out loud, gleefully explaining, "Your shower will have to wait because—"

Honey, knowing good and well he intended to announce her bath once again, pulled loose from Sawyer and stomped on Jordan's toe. Since he had on shoes and she didn't, he looked more surprised than hurt. He stared down at his foot, but then so did the rest of the men. They all looked as if they expected to see a bug to account for her attack. When no bug was found, all those masculine gazes transferred to her face, and she lifted her chin. Just because they were men didn't mean they had to wallow in insensitivity.

Jordan blinked at her, one brow raised high, and she quickly stepped back to Sawyer's side.

Her bravado wilted under Jordan's questioning gaze. Oh, God, she'd assaulted him! In his own home and in front of his family. Sawyer chuckled and put his arm around her.

Morgan stared at her with bad-tempered amusement. "Wanting a long soak, huh? I suppose I can use Gabe's shower..."

Casey stepped forward. "After me. I claimed it first."

"I'm older, brat."

"Doesn't matter!" And then Casey took off, racing for the shower. With a curse, Morgan started after him.

Honey wanted to slink back to bed and hide. The bath, which had sounded so heavenly moments before, now just seemed like a form of public humiliation. She was tired and her throat hurt and her head was beginning to ache. She turned to Sawyer, stammering, "I can wait."

Sawyer stared at her mouth.

Jordan stepped up and steered them both down the hall as if they were nitwits who needed direction. "Nonsense. Go take your soak. You'll feel better afterward." He limped pathetically as he walked, and Honey had the sneaking suspicion he did it on purpose, just to rattle her, not because she'd actually hurt him.

They were a strange lot—but she liked them anyway.

WARM WATER covered her to her chin, and she sighed in bliss. Finally, she felt clean again.

Where Sawyer had found the bubble bath, she didn't know, but she seriously doubted any of his brothers would lay claim to it. She smiled, wondering what they all thought of her. From the little bit she'd seen of them, they had a lot of similarities, yet they were each so different, too.

Of course, that might make sense considering their mother was evidently remarried. Honey couldn't imagine marrying once, much less twice. After the way her fiancé had used her, she wanted nothing to do with matrimony.

"You all right in there?"

"I'm fine. Go away."

"Just checking."

She smiled again. Sawyer had been hovering outside her door for the entire five minutes she'd been in the tub. He was something of a mother hen, which probably accounted for his chosen profession. He was meant to be a doctor. Everything about him spoke of a natural tendency to nurture. She liked it; she liked him. Too much.

The ultra-hot kiss... Well, she just didn't know what to think of it. Her lips still tingled and she licked them, savoring the memory of his taste. She'd almost married Alden, yet *he'd* never kissed her like that. And she'd certainly never thought about him the way she thought about Sawyer.

She'd known Alden two years and yet had never really wanted him. Not the way she wanted Sawyer after less than two days.

What would have happened if Jordan hadn't interrupted? Anything, nothing? She simply wasn't familiar enough with men to know. Not that familiarity would have helped, because she knew, even in her feverish state and even without a wealth of experience, Sawyer was different from most men. He was unique, a wonderful mix of pure rugged masculinity and incredible sensitivity.

He'd run the bathwater for her, placed a mat on the floor and fresh towels at hand and stacked her cleaned jeans and T-shirt on the toilet seat. All without mentioning the kiss and without getting too close to her. After he'd gotten everything ready, he'd looked at her, shook his head, then left with the admonition she should take as long as she liked, but not so long she got dizzy or overtired herself.

She intended to linger just a few minutes more. In all likelihood, the brothers would hold dinner for her. From all indications they enjoyed the novelty of having a woman underfoot and wouldn't pass up this opportunity to make her the center of attention again, as if she alone was the sole entertainment. She wasn't used to it, but she supposed she'd manage. For now, they were probably still organizing their own bath schedule, but how long would that take? Alden had always taken very short showers, his bathing a business, not a pleasure, whereas she'd always loved lingering in the water, sometimes soaking for hours.

She drained the tub and stepped out onto the mat. The steamy bath had relieved her throat some, and her muscles felt less achy after the soak. The towel Sawyer had provided was large and soft, and she wrapped herself in it, wishing she could just go back to bed and sleep for hours but knowing she wouldn't. She wanted to learn more about the brothers, she wanted to see the rest of the house and she needed to decide what to do.

She saw the edge of her peach panties showing from under the shirt, and she blushed. Somehow, the fact that Sawyer was now familiar with her underwear made their entire situation even more intimate, which meant more dangerous if she was honest with herself. How long would it take someone to figure out she was here? In a town this small, surely news traveled fast. Any strangers in town would have no problem finding her.

If she were smart, she'd forget her attraction to Sawyer, which weakened her resolve, and hightail it away as soon as possible.

"You about done in there?"

There was a slightly wary command to Sawyer's tone now. She grinned and called out, "Be right there. I'm getting dressed."

Silence vibrated between them, and Honey could

just imagine where his thoughts had gone. She bit her bottom lip. Sawyer was too virile for his own good.

She heard him clear his throat. "Do you need any help?"

She almost choked, but ended up coughing as she finished smoothing her T-shirt into place. She pulled the door open and said to his face, "Nope."

His gaze moved over her slowly, from the top of her head, where she had braided her long hair and then knotted it to keep it dry, to her T-shirt and down her jeans to her bare feet.

She bit her lip. "I don't know what happened to my sandals."

"Gone."

"Gone?"

He shook himself, then met her steady gaze. "Yeah. One fell off in the lake and sank. The other might still be in your car—I dunno. At the time, I wasn't overly worried about it, not with an unconscious woman in my arms."

"Ah."

"You're not wearing a bra."

"You can tell?" She quickly crossed her arms over her chest and started to go back into the bathroom to look for herself in the mirror. Sawyer caught her.

He slowly pulled her arms away and held them to her sides. She didn't stop him. Everything she'd just told herself about staying detached faded into oblivion under his hot, probing gaze.

There they stood in the middle of the hallway, only a foot apart, and somehow fear, sickness and worry didn't exist. All she could think of was whether or not he'd kiss her again, and if he found her satisfactory. She'd always been pleased with her body, but then, she wasn't a man.

In a hoarse tone, he noted, "You have goose bumps." Gently, his big, rough hands chaffed up and down her bare arms.

"The...the house is cold."

He lifted one broad shoulder. "We keep the air-conditioning pretty low this time of year. Men are naturally warmer than women. Especially when the woman is so slight. I'll get one of my shirts for you to put on."

Excitement at the way he watched her made it impossible to speak. She nodded instead.

"You two going to stand there all day gawking? I'm starved."

Sawyer swiveled his head to look at Gabe. He still held Honey's arms. "How can you be starving when you didn't do anything all day?"

"I cooked rolls this morning, fixed your leak, then visited three women. That's a busy day in anyone's book." He grinned, then asked, "Should I just drag the table in here so we can all gather in the hallway? Is that what we're doing?"

Sawyer narrowed his gaze at his brother, but there was no menace in the look. "I have an appointment with Darlene tomorrow so she can get her flu shot. Maybe I'll mention your fondness for Mississippi mud pie. I hear Darlene's quite a cook."

Gabe took a step back, his grin replaced with a look of pure horror. "You fight dirty, Sawyer, you know that?"

Honey was amazed at the amount of grudging respect in Gabe's tone, as if fighting dirty impressed him. And then he stomped away. Sawyer laughed.

She wondered if she would ever understand this unique clan of men. She looked up at Sawyer. "What in the world was that all about?"

A half smile tilted his mouth. "Darlene has the hots for Gabe and she's looking to get married. She's been chasing him pretty hard for awhile. Gabe has this old-fashioned sense of gallantry toward women, so he can't quite bring himself to come right out and tell her to leave him alone. He remains cautiously polite, and she remains determined."

"So if you mentioned a pie..."

"She'd be here every day with one." He grinned again and gently started her on her way. He moved slowly to accommodate her. The bath had tired her more than she wanted to admit, even to herself. Being sick or weak wasn't an easy concept to accept. Not for Honey.

"Why doesn't Gabe like her?"

"He likes her fine. She's a very attractive woman, beautiful even. Gabe went through school with her. I sometimes think that's the problem for him. He knows all the women around here so well. Gabe doesn't want to get serious about anyone, so he tries to avoid the women who are too obvious."

"Darlene's obvious?"

Sawyer shrugged. "Where Gabe's concerned, they all are. Darlene was just the first name to come to mind."

"Then she won't really be here tomorrow?"

"Nope." He put his arm around her waist and offered his support. "Come on, let's get that shirt and get to dinner so the savages can eat. If I leave them hungry too long, they're liable to turn on each other."

SAWYER WATCHED HER nibble delicately on her meal. And he watched his brothers watch her, amused that they were all so distracted by her. She looked uncomfortable with all the notice, but she didn't stomp on any more toes.

He doubted she had the energy for that. Her face was pale, her eyes dark with fatigue. Yet she refused to admit it. She had a lot of backbone, he'd give her that. As soon as she finished eating, he planned to tuck her back up in bed where she belonged.

He sat across from her—a deliberate choice so he *could* watch her. Gabe sat beside him, Casey sat beside her, with Morgan and Jordan at the head and foot of the table.

She'd been all round eyes and female amazement as she'd looked at the house on the way to the kitchen. Her appreciation warmed him. Most women who got through the front door were bemused with the styling of the house, all exposed pine and high ceilings and masculine functionality. The house wasn't overly excessive, but it was certainly comfortable for a family of large men. It had been his father's dream home, and his mother had readily agreed to it. At least, that's how she liked to tell it.

Sawyer grinned, because in truth, he knew there were few things his mother ever did readily. She was a procrastinator and liked to think things over thoroughly. Unlike his guest, who'd barreled through his fence and landed in his lake and then proceeded to try to slug him.

Sawyer noticed Morgan staring at him, and he wiped the grin off his face.

He returned his gaze to Honey and saw her look around the large kitchen. They never used the dining room, not for daily meals. But the kitchen was immense, one of the largest rooms in the house, and the place where they all seemed to congregate most often. For that reason they had a long pine table that could comfortably seat eight, as well as a short bar with three stools that divided the eating area from the cooking area. Pots hung on hooks, accessible, and along the outside wall there was a row of pegs that held everything from hats and jackets to car and truck keys. The entire house had black checked curtains at the windows, but the ones in the kitchen were never closed. With the kitchen on the same side of the house as his bedroom, there was always a view of the lake. His mother had planned it that way because, she claimed, looking at the lake made the chore of doing dishes more agreeable. After they'd gotten older and all had to take their turn, they'd agreed. Then they'd gotten a dishwasher, but still there were times when one or more of them would be caught there, drinking a glass of milk or snacking and staring at the placid surface of the lake.

Honey shifted, peeking up through her lashes to find a lot of appreciative eyes gazing at her. She glanced back down with a blush. She was an enticing mix of bravado and shyness, making demands one minute, pink-cheeked the next.

He liked seeing his shirt on her, this one a soft, worn flannel in shades of blue that did sexy things for her eyes. And he liked the way her heavy hair half tumbled down her nape, escaping the loose knot and braid, with silky strands draping her shoulders.

She didn't look as chilled, and he wondered if her nipples were still pebbled, if they pressed against his shirt.

His hand shook and he dropped his fork, taking the attention away from Honey. To keep his brothers from embarrassing him with lurid comments on his state of preoccupation, he asked Honey, "How come your car was filled with stuff, but no clothes?"

She swallowed a tiny bite of chicken and shrugged. She'd drunk nearly a full glass of tea but only picked at her food. "I left in a hurry. And that stuff was already in my car."

Sawyer glanced around and saw the same level of confusion on his brothers' faces that he felt.

Morgan pushed his empty plate away and folded his arms on the edge of the table. "*Why* was the stuff already in your car?"

She coughed, drank some tea, rubbed her forehead. Finally she looked at Morgan dead on. "Because I hadn't unloaded it yet." She aligned her fork carefully beside her plate and asked in her low, rough voice, "Why did you decide to become a sheriff?"

He looked bemused for just a moment, the customary scowl gone from his face. "It suited me." His eyes narrowed and he asked, "What do you mean you hadn't unloaded it? Unloaded it from where?"

"I'd just left my fiancé that very week. All I'd unloaded out of the car were my clothes and the things I needed right away. Before I could get the rest of the boxes out, I had to leave again. So the stuff was still in there. What do you mean, being a sheriff suits you? In what way?"

Her question was momentarily ignored while a silence as loud as a thunderclap hovered over the table. No one moved. No one spoke. All the brothers were watching Sawyer.

He drew a low breath. "She's not engaged anymore."

Gabe looked surprised. "She's not?"

"No."

"Why not?" Morgan demanded. "What happened?"

Before Sawyer could form an answer, Honey turned very businesslike. "What do you mean, being a sheriff suits you?"

A small, ruthless smile touched Morgan's mouth as he caught on to her game. He leaned forward. "I get to call the shots since I'm the sheriff. People have to do what I say, and I like it. Why did you leave your fiancé?"

"I found out he didn't love me. And what makes you think people have to obey you? Do you mean you lord your position over them? You take advantage?"

"On occasion. Did *you* love your fiancé?"

"As it turns out…no. What occasions?"

Morgan didn't miss a beat. "Like the time I knew Fred Barker was knocking his wife around, but she wouldn't complain. I found him drunk in town and locked him up. Every time I catch him drinking, I run him through the whole gambit of sobriety tests. And I find a reason to heavily fine him when I can't stick him in jail. He found out drinking was too expensive, and sober, he doesn't abuse his wife." He tilted his head. "If you didn't love the guy, why the hell were you engaged to him in the first place?"

"For reasons of my own. If you—"

"Uh-uh. Not good enough, honey. What reasons?"

"None of your business."

His voice became silky and menacing. "You're afraid to tell me?"

"No." She stared down her nose at him. Even with dark circles under her red-rimmed eyes and her hair more down than up, the look was effectively condescending. "I just don't like being provoked. And you're doing it deliberately."

Morgan burst out laughing—a very rare occurrence—and dropped back in his chair. The way Jordan and Gabe stared at him, amazed, only made him laugh harder.

Sawyer appreciated the quick way she turned the tables on his dominating brother. It didn't happen often, and almost never with women. Evidently, Morgan had been amused by her, too, because he could be the most ruthless bastard around when it suited him. Sawyer was glad he hadn't had to intervene. He wouldn't have let Morgan badger her, but he had been hoping Morgan could get some answers.

He found Honey could be very closemouthed when it suited her. It amazed him that she could look almost pathetically frail and weak one moment, then mean as a junkyard dog the next.

Gabe waved his fork. "Morgan does everything deliberately. It's annoying, but it does make him a good sheriff. He doesn't react off the cuff, if you know what I mean."

Jordan looked at Sawyer. "Not to change the subject—"

Morgan snorted. "As if you could."

"—but do we have anything for dessert?"

"Yeah." Sawyer watched Honey as he answered, aware of her new tension. She wasn't crazy about discussing her personal life, but he had no idea how much of it had to do with her claimed threats or the possibility of a lingering affection for her ex. His jaw tightened, and he practically growled, "Frosted brownies."

Jordan sat back. "They're no good?"

"They're fine. And in case none of you noticed, there's a new pig in the barnyard."

Honey started, the tension leaving her as confusion took its place. "A pig?"

"Yeah." Casey finished off a glass of milk, then poured another. He was a bottomless pit, and growing more so each day. "Some of the families can't afford to pay cash, so they pay Dad in other ways. It keeps us Adam's apple high in desserts, which is good, but sometimes we end up with more farm animals than we can take care of. We have horses, and they're no problem, but the goats and pigs and stuff, they can be a nuisance."

Jordan looked at Sawyer. "The Mensons could use a

pig. They had to sell off a lot of stock lately to build a new barn after theirs almost collapsed from age."

Sawyer continued to watch Honey, concerned that she was pushing herself too hard. At the moment, she didn't look ill so much as astonished. He grinned. Buckhorn was a step back in time, a close community that worked together, which he liked, but it would take some getting used to for anyone out of the area. "Feel free, Jordan. Hell, the last thing I want is another animal to take care of."

"They'll insist on paying something, but I'll make it real cheap."

"Trade for some of Mrs. Menson's homemade rock candy. Tell her I give it away to the kids when they come, and I'm nearly out."

"Good idea."

Honey looked around the table at all of them as Casey went to the counter to get the brownies. Her face was so expressive, even before she spoke, he knew she was worried. "You know everyone around here?"

With a short nod, Sawyer confirmed her suspicions. "We know them, and most people in the surrounding areas. Buckhorn only boasts seven hundred people, give or take a couple dozen or so."

Suddenly she blurted out, "Have you told anyone about me?" and Sawyer knew she was talking to everyone, not just him. What the hell was she so afraid of?

Casey dropped a brownie on the side of her plate, but she barely seemed to notice. Her hands were clenched together on the edge of the table while she waited for an answer.

"Dad told me not to say anything to anyone," Casey offered, when no one else spoke up. "So far, I'd say no one knows about you."

"Why do you care?" Sawyer waited, but he knew she wouldn't tell him a damn thing. "Is it because you think these people you claim want to hurt you might follow you here?"

Morgan, still lounging back in his chair, rubbed his chin. "I could run a check on you, you know."

She snorted over that. "If you can, then you already have. But you didn't find anything, did you?"

He shrugged, disgruntled by her response to what had amounted to a threat. She didn't threaten easily.

Jordan leaned forward. "You say someone is after you. Could it be this fiancé of yours?"

"Ex-fiancé," Sawyer clarified, then suffered through the resultant snorts and snickers from his demented brothers.

"I thought so at first. He...well, he wasn't happy that I broke things off. He was actually pretty nasty about it, if you want the truth."

"Truth would be nice."

She glared at Sawyer so ferociously, he almost smiled. But not quite.

"I think it wounded his pride or something," she explained. "But regardless of how he carried on, my father is certain it couldn't be him."

"Why?"

"If you'd ever met Alden, you'd know he doesn't have a physically aggressive bone in his body. He'd hardly indulge in a dangerous chase. He's ambitious, intelligent, one of my father's top men. And my father pointed out how concerned Alden is with appearances and that he'd hardly be the type to cause a scene or run the risk of making the news." She shrugged. "That's what my father likes most about him."

Sawyer curled his lip, more angered at her father's lack of support than anything else. "Alden? He sounds like a preppy."

"He *is* a preppy. Very into the corporate image and climbing the higher social ladder, though I didn't always know that. My father scoffed at the idea that Alden would chase me because regardless of his temper, I wouldn't be that important to him in his grand scheme of things."

He watched her face and knew she was holding something back, but what? Sawyer pushed her, hoping to find answers. "Even though you walked out on him?"

"I left, I didn't walk out."

"What the hell's the difference?"

She sighed wearily. "You make it sound like I staged a dramatic exit. It wasn't like that at all. I found out he didn't care about me, I packed up my stuff, wrote him a polite note and left."

Her body was tense, her expression carefully neutral. Sawyer narrowed his gaze. "Why did he ask you to marry him in the first place if he didn't care about you?"

She closed up on him, her face going blank, and Sawyer knew she still didn't trust him, didn't trust any of them. It made him so angry his hands curled into fists. He wasn't the violent type, but right now, he would relish one of Morgan's barroom brawls.

Sawyer surged to his feet to pace. He wanted to shake her; he wanted to pull her up against his body, feel her softness and kiss her silly again until she stopped resisting him, until she stopped fighting. He tightened his thighs, trying for an ounce of logic. "How in hell are we supposed to figure this out if you won't even answer a few simple questions?"

Morgan leaned back and stacked his hands behind his head. Jordan propped his chin on a fist. Gabe lifted one brow.

"You're not supposed to figure anything out." Honey drew a deep breath, watching him steadily. "You're just supposed to let me go."

6

SAWYER'S DARK EYES glittered with menace, and his powerful body tensed.

Watching him with an arrested expression, Morgan murmured, "Fascinating."

Jordan, also watching, said, "Shh."

Honey turned to Gabe, ignoring the other brothers, and especially Sawyer's astounding reaction to her refusal of help. She couldn't look at him without hurting, without wishing things could be different. She'd known him almost no time at all, yet she felt as if she'd known him forever. He'd managed, without much effort, to forge a permanent place in her memory. After she was gone, she'd miss him horribly.

Gabe grinned at her. It seemed they all loved to be provoking, but she wasn't up to another round. All the questions on Alden had shaken her. She'd tried to answer without telling too much, juggling her replies so that Sawyer might be appeased but at the same time wouldn't learn too much. Alden had been so vicious about her refusal to come back to him, to continue on with the marriage, she didn't dare involve anyone else in her troubles, especially not Sawyer, until she better understood the full risk, and why it existed in the first place.

She'd been looking blankly at Gabe for some time

now, and she cleared her throat. "Does your handy-man expertise extend to cars?"

"Sure."

Jordan kicked him under the table. Honey knew it, but in light of everything else they'd done, it didn't seem that strange or important.

While Gabe rubbed his shin and glared daggers at Jordan, Sawyer stalked over to her side of the table. With every pump of her heart, she was aware of him standing so close. She could feel his heat, breathe his scent, unique above and beyond the other brothers, who each pulsed with raw vitality. But her awareness, her female sensitivity, was attuned to Sawyer alone. Her skin flushed as if he'd stroked those large, rough hands down her body, when in fact he'd done no more than stand there, gazing down at her.

When she refused to meet his gaze, he propped both hands on his hips and loomed over her. "Gabe can fix your car, but you're not going anywhere until I'm sat-isfied that it's safe, which means you're going to have to quit stalling and explain some things."

Honey sighed again and tilted her head back to see him. Sawyer was so tall, even when standing she was barely even with his collarbone. Since she was sitting, he seemed as tall as a mountain. She really was tired of getting the third degree by overpowering men. "Saw-yer, how can I explain what I don't understand my-self?"

"Maybe if you'd just tell us what you do understand, we could come up with something that makes sense."

Leave it to a man to think he could understand what a woman couldn't. Her father had always been the same, so condescending, ready to discount her input on everything. And Alden. She shuddered at her own stupidity in ever agreeing to marry the pompous ass. Now that she'd met Sawyer and seen how caring a man could be...

With a groan she leaned forward, elbows on the table, and covered her face with her hands.

She was getting in too deep, making comparisons she shouldn't make. Morgan was right, he could start tracking her down. And since she didn't know what the threat was, only that it was serious, it was entirely possible he'd accidentally lead the threat to her—and to this family. She couldn't have that.

Car keys hung accessible on the wall by the back door. Sawyer wouldn't be sleeping in the same room with her tonight; there was no need. She'd have to take advantage of the opportunity. She'd borrow one of their vehicles, go into town and then get a bus ticket. She could leave a note telling Sawyer where to find his car.

Just the thought of leaving distressed her on so many levels, she knew she had to go as soon as possible, whether she felt up to it physically or not.

Sawyer evidently wanted her for a fling; he'd made his interest very obvious with that last kiss. He'd also indicated he found her to be a royal pain in the backside, and no wonder, considering she'd wrecked his fence and left a rusted car in his lake, along with taking his bed and keeping him up at night. When he wasn't watching her with sexual heat in his dark eyes, he was frowning at her with unadulterated frustration.

She felt the same incredible chemistry between

them, but she also felt so much more. He had the family life she'd always wondered about, the closeness and camaraderie, the sharing and support that she'd always believed to be a mere fairy tale. So often she'd longed for the life-style he possessed. And he was that special kind of man who not only accepted that life-style, but also contributed to it, a driving force in making it work for everyone.

She found Sawyer very sexually appealing, but he also felt safe and comforting. Security was a natural part of him, something built into his genetic makeup. And after the way her engagement had ended, she would never settle for half measures again, not when there was so much more out there.

She heard the shifting of masculine feet, a few rumbling questions, then Sawyer leaned down, his hand gently cradling the back of her head. "Honey?"

With new resolution she pushed her chair back, forcing Sawyer to move. "You're not going to let up on this, are you?"

Morgan snorted. Sawyer shook his head.

"All right." With an exaggerated sigh, she looked down, trying to feign weary defeat when inside she teemed with determination. "I'll tell you anything I can. But it's a long, complicated story. Couldn't it wait until the morning?"

She peeked up and caught Sawyer's suspicious frown. With a forced cough that quickly turned real, she said, "My throat is already sore. And I'm so tired."

Just that easily, Sawyer was swayed. He took her arm and helped her away from the table. "The morning will be fine. You've overdone it today."

By morning, she'd be long gone. And once she got to the next town, she'd contact her sister and let her know she was all right, then she could go with her original plan. She'd hire a private detective and pay him to figure out what was going on while she stayed tucked away, and those she cared about would stay safely uninvolved. She'd never forget this incredible family of men...but they would quickly forget her.

"Sawyer..." Morgan said in clear warning, obviously not pleased with the plan. Honey knew that particular brother couldn't care less if she was sick. Even though she wasn't really *that* sick, not anymore. But he didn't know it.

"It's under control, Morgan." Sawyer's tone brooked no arguments.

Morgan did hesitate, but then he forged on. "I know Honey's still getting over whatever ails her, but we really do need—"

With a loud gasp, she froze, then stiffened as his words sank in. Slowly, she turned to face Morgan. "You know my name."

There was no look of guilt on his hard, handsome face, just an enigmatic frown.

Sawyer shook his head in irritation while glaring at Morgan. "Around here, everything female is called honey."

Casey nodded. "We've got an old mule out in the field that Jordan named Honey because that's all she'd answer to."

She almost laughed at the sincerity on Casey's face, but instead she pulled free of Sawyer's hold and blazed an accusation. "He wasn't using an endearment. He was using *my name.*"

Morgan shrugged. "Honey Malone. Yeah, I went through your purse."

Her eyes widened. "You admit it? Just like that?" She nearly choked on resentment and coughed instead.

While Sawyer patted her on the back and Casey hurried to hand her a drink, Morgan said, "Why not?" He rolled his massive shoulders, not the least concerned with her ire. "You show up here under the most suspicious circumstances and you claim someone is trying to hurt you. Of course I wanted some facts. And how could I run that check on you if I didn't have your name? I thought you'd already figured that out."

Her mouth opened twice, but nothing came out. She should have realized he'd already gone through her things, only she'd been so busy trying to hold her own against him, and she'd taken his words as an idle threat, not a fait accompli. She was making a lot of stupid mistakes, trusting them all when she shouldn't.

Tonight. She had to leave tonight.

Then she remembered her bare feet and wanted to groan. She couldn't very well get on a bus without shoes. Maybe she could swipe a pair from Casey. She glanced at his feet and saw they were as large as Sawyer's. Good grief, she was in a house of giants.

Sawyer tipped up her chin. "He only looked in your wallet to find your name. He didn't go through every pocket or anything. Your privacy wasn't invaded any more than necessary. Your purse is in the closet in my room, if you want to check and make sure nothing is missing."

She ground her teeth together. "It isn't that." The last thing she was worried about was them stealing from her. She had little enough with her that was worth anything.

"Then what is it?"

She thought quickly, but trying to rationalize her behavior while the touch of Sawyer's hand still lingered on her face was nearly impossible. Everything about him set her off, but especially his touch. No matter where his fingers lingered, she felt it everywhere. "I...I don't have any shoes."

He frowned down at her bare feet for a long moment. "Are your feet cold?"

She wanted to hit him, but instead she turned away. Her brain was far too muddled to keep this up. If she didn't get away from him, she'd end up begging him to let her stay. "I'm going to bed now. Jordan, thank you for dinner."

He answered in his low, mesmerizing voice, no less effective for the shortness of his reply. "My pleasure."

She glanced at him. "I'd offer to help with the dishes, but I have the feeling—"

"Your offer would definitely be turned down." Sawyer released her, but added, "I'll be in to check on you in a few minutes."

The last thing she needed was to be tempted by him again. "No, thank you."

He stared at her hard, his gaze unrelenting. "In a few minutes, Honey, so do whatever it is you feel you have to do before going to bed. I left the antibiotics and the ibuprofen on the bathroom counter so you wouldn't forget to take them. After you're settled, I want to listen to your chest again."

There was a lot of ribald macho humor over that remark. Jordan choked down a laugh, and this time Gabe kicked him.

With a glare that encompassed them all, Honey stalked off. She was truly weary and wondering where in the world she was going to find shoes for her feet so she could steal a car and make her getaway from a group of large, overprotective, domineering men whom she didn't really want to leave at all.

Gads, life had gotten complicated.

HE KNOCKED on the door, but she didn't answer. Sawyer assumed she was mad and ignoring him, not that he'd let her get away with it. He opened the door just a crack—and saw the bed was empty. *She was gone.* His first reaction was pure rage, tinged with panic, totally out of proportion, totally unexpected. He shoved the door wide and stalked inside, and then halted abruptly when he saw her. His gut tightened and his heart gave a small thump at the picture she presented.

Honey sat on the small patio outside his room. She had her feet curled up on a chair, her head resting to the side, and she was looking at the lake. Or maybe she wasn't looking at anything at all. He couldn't see her entire face, only a small part of her profile. She looked limp, totally wrung out, and it angered him again when he thought of her stubbornness, her refusal to let him help her.

No one had ever refused his help. He was the oldest, and his brothers relied on him for anything they might need, including advice. Casey got everything from him that he had to give. Members of the community sought him out when they needed help either with a medical problem or any number of others things. He was a figurehead in the town, on the town council and ready and willing to assist. He gave freely, whatever the need might be, considering it his right, part and parcel with who and what he was. But now, this one small woman wanted to shut him out. *Like hell.*

Her physical impact on his senses was staggering. But it was nothing compared to the damn emotional impact, because the emotions were the hardest to fight and to understand. If it was only sex he wanted, he'd drive over the county limits and take care of the need. But he wanted *her* specifically, and it was making him nuts.

Being summer, it was still light out at eight o'clock, but the sun was starting to sink in the sky, slowly dipping behind a tree-topped hill across the lake. The last rays of sunshine sent fiery ribbons of color over the smooth surface of the water. A few ducks swam by, and far out a fish jumped.

Sawyer went back and closed the bedroom door silently, drawn to her though he knew he should just walk away. As he passed the bathroom, he noticed her toothbrush, still wet, on the side of the sink, along with a damp washcloth over the spigot, and his comb that he'd lent her. Those things looked strangely natural in his private domain, as if they belonged. She'd evidently prepared for bed, then was lured—as he often was—by the incredible serenity of the lake.

Though the house had a very comfortable covered

deck across the entire front and along one side by the kitchen, he'd still insisted on adding the small patio off his bedroom. In the evening, he often sat outside and just watched the night, waiting for the stars or the clouds to appear, enjoying the way mist rose from the lake to leave lingering dew on everything. The peacefulness of it would sink into his bones, driving away any restlessness. Many times his son or one of his brothers would join him. They didn't talk, they just sat in peace together, enjoying the closeness.

He'd never shared a moment like this with a woman, not even his wife.

He approached Honey on silent feet. She looked melancholy and withdrawn, and for a long time he simply took in the sight of her. He'd seen her looking fatigued with illness and worry, and he'd seen her eyes snapping with anger or panic. He'd watched her cheeks warm with a blush, her brow pucker with worry over his son. He'd even seen her muster up her courage to embrace a verbal duel with Morgan. Sawyer had known her such a short time, but in that time, he had truly related to her. Whereas hours might be spent on a date, her health had dictated they bypass the cordial niceties of that convention, and their relationship had been intimate from the first. The effects were devastating. He'd already spent more time in her company than most men would through weeks of dating.

Every facet of her personality enthralled him more than it should have. He wanted to see her totally relaxed, without a worry, finally trusting him to take care of her and make things right.

And most of all, he wanted to see her face taut with

fierce pleasure as he made love to her, long and slow and deep.

He slid the French door open, and she looked at him.

There were two outdoor chairs on his private patio, and he pulled one close to her. He spoke softly in deference to the quiet of the night and the quiet in her blue eyes. "You look pensive."

"Hmm." She turned to stare back out at the lake, tilting her head at the sound of the crickets singing in the distance. "I was...uneasy. But this is so calming, like having your problems washed away. It's hard to maintain any energy out here, even for irritation."

"You shouldn't be irritated just because we want to help."

Her golden brown lashes lowered over her eyes. "Dinner with your family was...interesting. Around our house, there was only my sister and me. It was always quiet, and if we talked, it was in whispers because the house was so silent. Dinner wasn't a boisterous event."

"We can take a little getting used to."

She smiled. "No, I enjoyed myself. The contrast was wonderful, if that makes any sense."

That amused him, because meals at home were always a time to laugh and grouse and share. She'd probably find a lot of contrasts, and he hoped she enjoyed them all. But it also made him sad, thinking of how lonely her life must have been. "It makes perfect sense," he assured her.

"Good."

Because it had surprised him, he added, "You held your own with my brothers."

She laughed, closing her eyes lazily. "Yes. Morgan is a bully, but I have the feeling he's fair."

Sawyer considered her words and the way she'd spoken them. "Honorable might be a better word. Morgan can be very unfair when he's convinced it's for the best. He's a no-holds-barred kind of man when he's got a mission."

Her long blond hair trailed over her shoulder all the way to her thigh, catching the glow of the setting sun as surely as the lake did. She tilted her chin up to a faint warm breeze, and his blood rushed at the instinctively feminine gesture and the look of bliss on her face. "It was so cold inside," she whispered, "I wanted to feel the sunshine. I came out here to warm up, then couldn't seem to make myself go back in."

They did keep the air low, but not so much that she should be uncomfortable. He reached over and placed his palm on her forehead, then frowned. "You could be a little feverish again. Did you take the ibuprofen I left in the bathroom?"

"Yes, I did. And the antibiotic." She blinked her eyes open and sighed. "Did I thank you for taking such good care of me, Sawyer?"

A low thrumming started in his veins, making his body throb. He could feel his own heartbeat, the acceleration of his pulse—just because she'd said his name. "I don't know, but it isn't necessary."

"To me it is. Thank you."

He swallowed down a groan. He wanted to lift her onto his lap and hold her for hours, just touching her, breathing in her spicy scent, which kept drifting to him in subtle, teasing whiffs. Right now, she smelled of sunshine and warmth and the musky scent of woman, along with a fragrance all her own, one that seemed to be seeping into his bones. It drove him closer to the edge and made him want to bury himself in the unique scent.

But beyond that, he wanted to strip her naked and settle her into his bed. He wanted to look his fill, to feel her slender thighs wrap tight around his hips, her belly pressed to his abdomen, her body open and accepting as he pushed inside for a nice long slow ride, taking his time to get her out of his blood.

He wanted to comfort her and he wanted to claim her, conflicting emotions that left him angry at his own weakness.

He was aware of her watching him, and then she said, "Can I ask you a few questions?"

He laughed, and the sound was a bit rusty with his growing arousal. "I'd have to be a real bastard to say no, considered how my brothers and I have questioned you tonight."

She sent him an impish smile. "True enough." She curled her legs up a little higher then rested her cheek on her bent knees. "Why did Morgan really become a sheriff?"

That wasn't at all what he'd been expecting, and her interest in his brother brought on a surge of annoyance. "You think there's a secret reason?"

"I think there's a very personal reason." She shooed a mosquito away from her face, then resettled herself. "And I'm curious about him."

Sawyer felt himself tense, though he tried to hide it. "Curious, as in he's a man and you're a woman?"

She looked at his mouth. "No. Curious as in he's your brother, and therefore a part of you."

Satisfied, his twinge of unreasonable jealousy put to rest, Sawyer turned to look at the lake. "There's no denying our relationship, is there? Morgan and I share a lot of the same features, even though he is a bit of an overgrown hulk. Except I have my father's eyes, and he has my mother's."

"You look alike more so than the other two."

"We had a different father. Our father died when Morgan was just a baby."

"Oh." She shifted, unfolding her long legs and sitting upright. She reached over and touched his arm, just a gentle touch with the tips of her fingers, lightly stroking, but the effect on his body was startling. He felt that damn stroke in incredible places.

"I'm sorry," she whispered. "I had thought your mother just divorced."

He covered her hand with his own to still the tantalizing movement. "She was that, too."

"But..."

To keep the emotions she evoked at bay, he launched into a dispassionate explanation. "She married Jordan's father when I was five, and divorced him shortly after Jordan was born. I barely remember him, but he lost his job after the marriage and he started drinking. It became a problem. At first my mother tried to help him through it, but she would only tolerate so much in front of her children, and he couldn't seem to help himself, or so she's said. So she left him. Or rather, she divorced him and he took off and we never hear from him. My mother never requested child support, and he never stayed around long enough to offer it."

"Oh, God. Poor Jordan."

"Yeah. He wasn't much more than an infant when they divorced, so he didn't know his father at all. He's never mentioned him much. He was always a quiet kid. Morgan loved to beat up the boys who gave Jordan any grief. We both used to try to protect him. We sort of understood that he was different, quiet but really intense."

"He's not so quiet now." She made a face, wrinkling her nose, probably remembering the way Jordan had teased her about her bath. "He's not as demanding as Morgan, but I wouldn't exactly call him shy."

"No. He's not shy." Sawyer smiled, thinking of how she'd stomped on Jordan's foot. "None of my brothers are. But Jordan isn't as outgoing as the others, either."

"When did he change?" An impish light twinkled in her eyes. "After his first girlfriend?"

She was teasing, and Sawyer liked that side of her, too. "Actually, it happened when he was only ten. He found some kids tormenting a dog. He told them to leave the dog alone, and instead, one boy threw a rock at it. The dog, a really pitiful old hound, let out a yelp, and Jordan went nuts on the boys." Sawyer chuckled, remembering that awesome day. "He was like a berserker—impressed the hell out of everyone who watched."

Honey shook her head. "Males are so impressed by the weirdest things."

Sawyer glanced at her. "This wasn't weird! It was life-altering stuff. Sort of a coming-of-age kinda thing.

My mother had always taught us to be good to animals, and Jordan couldn't bear to see the old dog harassed. The boys were two years older than Jordan, and there were three of them. Morgan and I were on the sidelines, waiting to jump in if we needed to, but being so much older, we couldn't very well start brawling with twelve-year-olds."

"Too bad they weren't older."

He heard her impudent wit, but pretended she was serious. "Yeah. Neither of us is fond of idiots who abuse animals. We wouldn't have minded a little retribution of our own. But Jordan held his ground and did a good job of making his point. He ended up with a black eye, a couple dozen bruises, and he needed stitches in his knee. My mother liked to have a fit when she saw him. And Morgan and I got lectured for hours for not stopping the fight. But no one messed with Jordan again after that. And anytime an animal was hurt or sick, someone would tell Jordan. I swear, that man can whisper an animal out of an illness."

"So that started him on the road to being a vet. What made Morgan decide to be a sheriff?"

Sawyer turned her hand over and laced his fingers with hers. Her hands were small, slender, warm. Along the shore of the lake, a few ducks waddled by then glided effortlessly into the water, barely leaving a ripple. Peonies growing on the other side of the house lent a sweet fragrance to the air, mixing with her own enticing scent.

He was horny as hell, and she wanted to talk about his brothers.

"Morgan is a control freak," he managed to say around the restriction in his throat.

"I noticed."

Since she'd been a recipient of his controlling ways, he supposed she had. "He used to get into a lot of scrapes, sort of a natural-born brawler. Give him a reason to tussle and he'd jump on it. He got in trouble a few times at school, and my mother was ready to ground him permanently. Gabe's dad was a good influence on him."

Honey started. "Your mother was married three times?"

Sawyer didn't take offense at her surprise. No one had been more surprised by that third marriage than his mother herself. "Yeah." He smiled, dredging up fond memories. "I was eight years old when Brett Kasper started hanging around. My mother wanted nothing to do with him, and I'd ask her why, since he was so obviously trying to get in good with her and he was a nice guy and *we* all liked him—even Morgan. Brett would offer to clean out her gutters, play baseball with us, run to open doors for her. But he was always honest about why he did it. He'd tell us he was wooing our mother and ask for our help." Sawyer laughed. "We'd all talk about him to her until finally she'd threaten to withhold dessert if we mentioned his name again. I now understand how burned she felt, losing her first husband in the military, divorcing her second husband as a mistake."

"Because you went through a divorce, too?"

He wouldn't get into that with her. The divorce

hadn't bothered him that much, unfortunately. It was all the deceit that had changed his life.

Sawyer shrugged. "My mother worked damn hard to keep everything going, raising four sons, working, keeping up the house. My father's pension helped, even paid for a lot of my college. And we all pitched in, but it wasn't easy for her."

"She must be incredible."

"Brett used to say she was as stubborn as an aged mule and twice as ornery."

"What a romantic."

Sawyer laughed. "He didn't cut her any slack, which is good because my mother is strong and she wouldn't want a man who couldn't go toe to toe with her. Brett wanted her and he went after her, even though she was gun-shy and didn't want to take another chance. Sometimes she was rude as hell to him. But Brett was pushy and he kept hanging around until he finally wore her down."

Honey gave him a dreamy smile. "A real happy ending."

"Yeah. They've been married twenty-eight years now. Brett's great. I love him. He's always treated us the same, as if he'd fathered the lot of us. Even Morgan, who can be so damn difficult."

"You said he helped Morgan?"

"He helped redirect Morgan's more physical tendencies by signing him up for boxing. And he set up a gym of sorts in the basement, which we all used until Gabe moved down there. Now there's just a weight room in what is supposed to be a den. My mother frets every time she sees it."

Honey laughed again, a low, husky sound that vibrated along his nerve endings and made him acutely aware of how closely they sat together, their isolation from the others, the heaviness of the humid summer air. He reacted to it all and kissed her knuckles before he could stop himself.

Just that brief touch made him want so much more.

Trying to regroup, he said, "Morgan chose to be a sheriff because he likes control, and for him, that's the ultimate control. But regardless of what he says, it isn't control over other people, it's control of himself. He knows he's more wild than not, that he'll always be more aggressive than most people. Choosing to run for sheriff was his way of forcing himself to be in control at all times."

She gave a very unladylike snort. "I think he's a big fraud."

Her misperceptions prompted Sawyer to grin. He could just tell she and Morgan would butt heads again and again if they spent much time around each other.

Of course, that was iffy, with her planning to leave and him planning to eventually let her.

"The hell of it is, Morgan never starts fights, he just finishes them. With that scowl of his, he can bring on a lot of attitude that men, especially bullies, generally object to. And to be fair, he always gives the other guy a chance to back off, but there's that gleam in his eyes that taunts. Morgan's always had an excess of energy and he gets edgy real quick. So to burn up energy, he either fights or he..." Appalled at what he'd almost said, Sawyer stemmed his ridiculous outpouring of personal confidences, wondering if he'd already stepped over the line. He was so comfortable with her, a fact he'd only realized, and she was so damn easy to talk to, he'd completely forgotten himself.

She tilted her head, her eyes alight with curiosity. "Or what?"

"Never mind."

"Oh, no, you don't!" She shook her head even as she fought off a yawn. "No way. You can't just tease me like that and then not tell me."

She looked sleepy and warm and piqued, all at once. Again he felt that unfamiliar rush of lust and tenderness and knew he was reacting to her when he shouldn't. But he just couldn't help himself. She drew him in without even trying.

Caught by her gaze, he admitted in a hoarse tone, "Morgan either fights...or he makes love. Either way, he burns off energy."

Her cheeks immediately colored and her eyes widened. "Oh. Yeah, I guess...I guess that could work."

Having caught her uncertainty, Sawyer leaned forward to see her averted face. "You don't sound certain."

She cleared her throat. "Well, it's not like...that is..." She peeked at him, her brow furrowed in thought. "Is it?"

Sawyer stared at her, blank-brained for just a moment, then he surged to his feet. Damn, if she was asking him if sex was really all that vigorous, he didn't think he could suffice with a mere verbal answer. Surely a woman as sexy, as attractive as she would already know! Damn her, she plagued his brain with her contradictions, her looks earthy and sensual, her behavior so modest. Bold one minute, timid the next.

He stared down at the lake for long moments, trying to get himself together and fight off the surge of lust that swamped him. He heard her stand behind him.

"Sawyer?"

"What?" He didn't mean to sound so brusque, but it felt as if she were killing him and his resolve by small degrees. Torturous, but also extremely erotic.

"Can I ask you something?"

Her tone was hesitant and shy, and he prayed her question wouldn't be about sex. He was only human, and she was too much temptation.

He looked at her over his shoulder and tried to dampen his frustration. "What is it with all these questions? I thought your throat was sore."

"It is. But your family is so different, so special. It's the way I always thought families should be. I've enjoyed hearing about them. And I have had a few things vexing my mind."

A grin took him by surprise; she sounded so worried. "Vexing you, huh?"

"Yes."

"All right." Turning, he gave her his full attention. The setting sun did amazing things to her fair hair and her blue eyes while making her skin appear even smoother. It was still hot and humid outside, even though it was evening, and she'd removed his shirt. He could visually trace the outline of her breasts beneath the T-shirt, the full shape of them, the roundness, even the delicate jut of her nipples. His abdomen pulled tight in an effort to fight off the inevitable reaction in his body, but he still felt himself harden. He could see the narrowness of her midriff, the dip of her waist. She hadn't tucked the T-shirt in, and still the flare of her hips was obvious and suggestive.

She shaded her eyes with a small hand and blurted, "Why did you kiss me?"

Taken completely off guard, he blinked at her. After a moment, he said, "Come again?"

"Earlier." She bit the side of her mouth and shifted nervously. "When you kissed me. Why'd you do it?"

She had to ask? He was thirty-six years old, had been kissing females since he was twelve, and yet none of them had ever asked him such a thing. Trying to figure out what she was thinking, he countered her question with one of his own. "Why do you think I did it?"

She looked so young when she turned bashful. He wondered at the man who'd given her up, who hadn't really loved her, as she'd put it. Sawyer had already decided he was a damn fool. Now, seeing her like this, he was glad. She deserved better than a fool, better than a man who'd be stupid enough to let her go.

He stepped closer, so tempted to kiss her again, to show her instead of tell her about her appeal. But he knew it wasn't right, that he was taking advantage of her situation and confusion. She stared down at her bare feet. "My sister always told me I was pretty."

He wanted to see her eyes, but no matter how he willed it, she wouldn't look up. "You're very pretty. But I hardly kiss every pretty woman I see." And in truth, he'd known women much more beautiful. They simply hadn't interested him; they didn't draw him as she did. "Besides," he added, trying for some humor, "your face is bruised, and your lips are chapped, and there's dark circles under your eyes."

"Oh." She touched her cheeks, then let her hands drop away with a frown.

He waited while she thought about that. "Alden used to tell me I was shaped...okay."

"Okay?"

She gave a grave nod. "Men can be...enticed, by physical stuff, I know."

She was attempting to sound blasé, and he barely held back his laugh. Alden must have been a complete and total putz. She was much better off without him. "Honey, you're sexy as hell, and sure, to some men that's all that matters, but again—" He gave a philosophical shrug.

"You don't kiss every sexy woman you see?"

"Exactly."

She licked her lips, and her expression was earnest, if reserved. "So then why did you?"

Very softly, he admitted, "I shouldn't have."

"That doesn't answer my question."

Her cheek was sun-warmed beneath his palm as he tilted up her face, determined to see her eyes, to read her. Besides, he couldn't seem to *not* touch her. "What's your real question, sweetheart?"

Her eyes darkened, and the pulse in her throat raced, but she didn't look away this time. She fidgeted, shifting from one foot to the next. "Did...did you think since I was available, but determined not to be here too long, you could just...you know. Have a quick fling?"

He couldn't remember the last time he'd smiled so much. But she amused and delighted him with her every word—when she wasn't provoking him and pricking his temper. She was both the most open, honest woman he'd ever met, sharing her feelings and emotions without reserve or caution, and the most stubbornly elusive, refusing to tell him any necessary truths. "Anyone who knows me could tell you I'm hardly the type for a quick indiscreet fling, or any kind of fling. But certainly not with someone who didn't want the same."

She looked startled. "You think I don't want—"

Interrupting that thought seemed his safest bet. "I don't think you know what you want right now. But it surely isn't to be used."

Her eyes narrowed in suspicion. "Meaning?"

"Meaning I'm human, and I get restless like any other man. But I have a reputation here, and a lot of people look up to me. I have to be very circumspect."

She stared at him, her expression almost awed that such sanctimonious words had escaped his mouth. He felt like an idiot. "Honey, I'm sorry, but I just can't—"

She took an appalled step back. "I wasn't asking you to!"

His mouth quirked again, but he ruthlessly controlled it. "When I get too restless, there are women I know *outside* of town who feel just as turned off by commitment as I do. They're content with physical release and no strings."

Her mouth formed an O.

Feeling aggrieved, he explained, "They're *nice* women, who are content with their lives, but they get lonely. The world being what it is, it's not easy to find someone respectable who isn't looking for marriage. We suit, and it's simple and convenient and—"

Her face was bright red. He couldn't believe he'd gotten into this.

"I see. So you...indulge yourself with these women you don't really care about. But I don't fall in that category?"

His teeth clicked together. He wanted to shake her. He wanted to haul her up close and nestle his painful erection against her soft belly. He shook his head, as much for himself as for her. "You most definitely don't fall into that category. You're young and confused and scared. You're not from around here and you don't know me well enough to know I have no desire to remarry. And that's why I said I shouldn't have kissed you." He shoved his hands into his pockets and took a determined step away. "It won't happen again, so you don't have to worry about it."

She drew a long, considering breath. "I wasn't worried. Not really. I just wasn't sure..." She bit her lip and then blurted, "Most of the time you don't seem to like me very much. You feel responsible for some dumb reason, and you're kind enough, but...I just wasn't sure what to think about the kiss."

She obviously had no experience with aroused men, to mistake his personal struggles for dislike. And no sooner did he have that thought than he tried to squelch it. It was dangerous territory and would lead him into more erotic thoughts of what he'd like to show her, and just how much he liked her. Instead of explaining, he said, "I'd like you a whole lot more if you'd stop keeping secrets."

She got her back up real quick, turning all prickly on him. "We agreed we'd talk in the morning."

"So we did." He was more than ready to let it drop before he dug himself in too deep. "Why don't you head on in." If she stood there looking at him even a minute more, he was liable to forget his resolve and gather her close and kiss her senseless—despite all the damn assurances he'd just given her. These uncontrollable tendencies had never bothered him before; now he felt on the ragged edge, like a marauder about to break under the restraint. The things he wanted to do to her didn't bear close scrutiny. "You look ready to drop," he quickly added, hoping she wouldn't argue.

Sighing, she turned to go in. "I feel ready to drop."

Sawyer followed her through the door. The cold air-conditioning was a welcome relief as it washed against his heated skin. It may be evening, but summer in Kentucky meant thick humidity and temperatures in the nineties, sometimes even through the night.

Honey came to an abrupt halt beside the bed and stared at the fresh linens. "Someone changed the bed."

"I did. I figured you'd want clean sheets."

She gave him a querulous frown for reasons he couldn't begin to fathom, then sat on the edge of the mattress and reached for the cat. Until she did so, Sawyer hadn't realized the cat was back. Her calico coloring made her blend perfectly with the patchwork quilt.

Honey lifted the cat onto her lap and stroked her, being especially careful with her bandaged tail. "So I know you won't kiss me again, but I still don't know why you did in the first place."

Watching her pet the cat mesmerized him—until she

spoke, breaking the spell with her unsettling question. He didn't want to answer her because he knew it would somehow complicate things further. But she had that stubborn, set look again, and he figured she wouldn't go to bed until he satisfied her curiosity. He crossed his arms over his chest and studied her while searching for the right words. "I kissed you because I couldn't seem to stop myself."

"But why?"

He growled, "Because you're quick-witted and sweet and you have more courage than's good for you. And you're stubborn and you make me nuts with your secrets." Almost reluctantly, he admitted, "And you smell damn good."

She stared up at him, bemused. "You kissed me because I annoy you with my stubbornness and...and my *courage?*"

He gave a sharp nod. "And as I said, you're smart and you smell good. Incredibly good."

"But I thought—"

"I know what you thought." She'd complained about smelling like the lake when to him, she'd smelled like herself, a woman he wanted.

He started to ask her why she'd kissed him back, because she had. She'd nearly singed his eyebrows with the way she'd clung to him, how her mouth had moved under his, the way she'd greedily accepted his tongue, curling her own around it.

He shuddered, then headed for the door, escape his only option. Somehow he knew he'd be better off not knowing what had motivated her. "I won't sleep in here tonight, but if you need anything just let me know. I'm using the front bedroom."

She rushed to her feet. "I hadn't thought...I didn't mean to chase you out of your own room!"

There was so much guilt in her face, he slowed for just a heartbeat. "You didn't chase me out. I just figured since you were already settled..."

"I'll switch rooms." She took an anxious step toward him. "You shouldn't have to be inconvenienced on my account."

He hesitated a moment more, caught between wanting to reassure her and knowing he had to put distance between them. "It's not a problem. Good night."

She started to say something else, but he pulled the door shut. Truth was, he liked knowing she was in his bed. He didn't know if he'd ever be able to sleep there again without thinking of her—and dreaming.

7

THE HOUSE was eerily quiet as she slipped the bedroom door open, using only the moonlight filtering in through the French doors to guide her way. Though she hadn't lied about being exhausted, she hadn't slept. The clean sheets no longer smelled of Sawyer's crisp, masculine scent. She'd resented the loss.

She listened with her ear at the crack in the door, but there was nothing. Everyone was in bed, as she'd suspected, probably long asleep. She pictured Sawyer, on his back, his long body stretched out, hard, hot. Her heart gave an excited lurch.

He'd kissed her because she was smart.

And sweet and stubborn and... She'd wanted to cry when he'd given those casual compliments. She'd almost married a man who'd never even noticed those things about her, and if he had, he wouldn't have found them attractive. For him, her appeal had been based on more logical assets, what she could bring him in marriage, her suitability as a partner, the image she'd project as his wife.

Occasionally he'd told her she was lovely, and he'd had no problem using her body. But nothing he'd ever done, not even full intimacy, had been as hot, as exciting, as Sawyer's kiss. God, she'd been a fool to almost marry Alden.

Her father had once claimed she could have any husband she wanted based on her looks and his financial influence, neither of which she'd ever considered very important. Sawyer couldn't be interested in her father's influence, because he didn't know about it and didn't need it, in any case. And from what he'd said, he didn't find her all that attractive. She smiled and touched her cheek. She was a wreck, and she didn't even care. He'd kissed her, and he'd told her she smelled good, and he liked her wit and stubbornness and courage. Such simple compliments that meant so much. Without even realizing it, he'd given her a new perspective on life, a new confidence. She'd no longer doubt her own worth or appeal, thanks to his grudging admission.

She knew she had to leave before she threw herself at him and begged him to pretend she was one of the women from outside of town. Every time she was around him, she wanted him more.

She'd left a note on the bed, made out to Sawyer and sealed in a bank deposit envelope she'd found on his dresser. It was a confession of sorts, explaining how she felt and part of the reasons she had to leave. It was embarrassing, but she felt she owed him that much, at least. She knew he wouldn't be happy with her furtive defection, but from what he'd said, he'd be even less happy if she lured him into an intimacy he was bound and determined to resist.

Her purse had been in the closet, as the brothers had claimed, and all her credit cards and I.D. were still inside. She was ready to go.

The door was barely open when the small cat leaped

off the bed to follow her out. When Honey reached for the cat, meaning to close her back in the bedroom so she wouldn't make any noise, the cat bounded out of reach. Honey wasn't sure what to do, but it was certain she couldn't waste time hunting for the animal in the dark. She'd been through the house, but she wasn't familiar enough with the setup to launch a search; odds were she'd knock something over.

She was halfway down the hallway, moving slowly and silently though the blackness, when the cat meowed. Every hair on her body stood on end while she waited, frozen, for some sign she'd been discovered. Nothing. The brothers slept on.

Honey glared behind her, but could only see two glowing green eyes in the darkness. Again she reached for the cat; again it avoided her. She felt the brush of soft fur as the cat moved past, then back again, always just out of reach. Honey cursed silently and prayed the cat would be quiet, and that she wouldn't trip on it and knock anything over.

The house was so large, it took her some time to make her way to the kitchen, especially with the cat winding around her ankles every few steps. She'd always liked cats, but now she was thinking of becoming a dog woman.

A tiny, dim light on the stove gave scant illumination across the tiled kitchen floor. She could barely see, but she knew the keys were hanging on a peg on the outside wall, close to the door, so she used the stove light as a compass of sorts, helping her to orient herself to the dark room. Shuffling her feet to avoid tripping on unseen objects, including felines, she made her way

over to the door, trying to avoid the heavier shadows
of what she assumed to be the table and counter. Once
her searching hand located the keys, she had another
dilemma. There were too many of them!

Her heart pounded so hard it was almost deafening.
Her palms were sweaty, her stomach in a tense knot.
The damn cat kept twining around her bare feet, me-
owing, making her jumpy. She had no idea where the
pet food was kept and had no intention of trying to
find out.

Finally, knowing she had to do something or she'd
definitely faint, she ignored the cat and decided to take
all the keys. When she found one that operated the
closest vehicle, she'd drop the rest in the grass, leaving
them behind.

She tucked her purse under her arm and wiped her
sweaty palms on her jeans. Carefully, shuddering at
every clink and rattle, she lifted the various key rings.
There were five sets. She swallowed hard and, clutching the keys in one hand, her purse in the other, she
reached for the kitchen door. The cat looked up and
past her, meowed, then sprinted away. Honey turned
to see where the cat was headed and barely caught
sight of a large, looming figure before a growling voice
took her completely off guard.

"You were actually going to steal my car!"

She jerked so hard, it felt like someone had snapped
her spine. At first, no sound escaped her open mouth
as she struggled to suck in air, then her heartbeat re-
sumed in a furious trot, and she shrieked involuntarily.
Shrill. Loud. The cat took exception to her noise, and
with a hiss, darted out of the room. Honey seriously

thought her heart might punch right through her chest, it was racing so frantically. It didn't matter that the voice was familiar; she'd been sure she was all alone, being incredibly sneaky, and then he was there. The sets of keys fell from her limp hand in a clatter on the tile floor. Her purse dropped, scattering the contents everywhere.

Sawyer was there in an instant, his hands clasping her shoulders and jerking her around to face him, hauling her up close on her tiptoes again. Her body flattened against his, and she could feel his hot angry breath on her face, feel the steel hardness of his muscles, tensed for battle.

"You were going to steal my goddamn car!"

"No..." The denial was only a whisper. She still couldn't quite catch her breath, not after emptying her lungs on that screech.

He took one step forward, and her back came up against the door while his body came up against her front. "If I hadn't been sitting there in the shadows, you'd be sneaking out right now." He shook her slightly. "Admit it."

She swallowed, trying to find her tongue. Instead, the damn tears started. He'd been there all along? She'd never stood a chance? She sniffed, fighting off the urge to weep while trying to decide what to say, how to defuse his rage.

She trembled all over, and she couldn't find the willpower to explain. She felt Sawyer practically heaving, he was so angry, and in the next instant he groaned harsh and low and his hands were on her face, his thumbs brushing away the tears, his mouth hungrily searching for hers. The relief was overwhelming.

She cried out and wrapped her arms around him. He'd said it wouldn't happen again, that not only didn't he want her for a fling, he didn't want her for anything. She'd told herself that was for the best. She'd told herself she hadn't cared. But inside, she'd crumbled.

Now he wanted her, and she was so weak with fear and excitement, all she could do was hold on to him.

One of his hands slid frantically down her side, then up under her shirt. He bit her bottom lip gently and when she opened her mouth, his tongue thrust inside, just as his long, hot fingers closed over her breast.

She jerked her mouth away to moan at the acute pleasure of it—and the kitchen light flashed on.

Blinded, Honey shaded her eyes while Sawyer jerked her behind him and turned to face the intruder.

"Just what the hell is going on?" There was two seconds of silence, then, "Ah. Never mind. Stupid question. But why the hell is she screaming about it?"

Morgan's voice. *Oh, my God, oh my God, oh, my God.* Honey peeked around Sawyer, then yelped. Good grief, the man was buck naked and toting a gun!

Sawyer shoved her back behind him again with a curse. "Damn it, Morgan, put the gun away."

"Since it's just you, I will. That is, I would if I had any place to put it." Honey could hear his amusement, and she moaned again.

Sawyer muttered a low complaint. "You could have at least put some shorts on."

"If I'd known you were only romping in the kitchen

I would have! But how the hell was I supposed to know? She *screamed*, Sawyer. I mean, I know you're rusty and all, but damn. You must have completely lost your touch."

Honey clutched at Sawyer's back, her hot face pressed to his bare shoulder. This couldn't be happening.

Sawyer crossed his arms over his chest. "She screamed because I caught her trying to steal the car keys." He kicked a set toward Morgan. The sound of them skidding over the floor was almost obscene. Honey didn't bother to look to see if Morgan picked them up. The man was blatantly, magnificently naked, and didn't seem to care. She shuddered in embarrassment and burrowed closer against Sawyer, pressing her face into his hot back, trying to blot the vision from her mind.

Morgan gave a rude grunt. "I see. She was stealing one of our cars. And so you kissed her to stop her?"

"Don't be a smart ass."

Suddenly she heard Casey say, "What's going on? I heard someone scream."

Honey thought if there was any luck to be had for her, she would faint after all. She waited, praying for oblivion, and waited some more, but no, she remained upright, fully cognizant of the entire, appalling predicament she'd gotten herself into.

Sawyer's body shifted as he gave a heavy sigh. "It's all right, Casey. Honey was just trying to sneak off in the night. She was going to steal a car."

"I was not!" Honey couldn't bear the thought of Sawyer's son believing such a thing about her. She cautiously peeked around Sawyer and saw Jordan and Gabe amble into the room. *Just what she needed.* Morgan, bless his modest soul, had sat down behind the bar. All she could now see of him was his chest. But that was still more than enough, especially since the gun remained in his hand, idly resting on the bar counter.

Gabe held up a hand. "I already heard the explanations. Damn, but she has a shrill scream. I had to scrape myself off the ceiling, it startled me so bad."

Jordan held the cat in the crook of one arm, gently soothing it. "I even heard her all the way out in the garage. When I got here, the poor cat was nearly hysterical."

Ha! Honey eyed them all, especially that damn traitor feline, and tried to muster up a little of that courage Sawyer claimed she had. At least they weren't *all* naked, she told herself, then shuddered with relief. Casey had pulled on jeans, and Gabe had on boxers. Jordan had a sheet wrapped around himself, held tight at his hip with a fist.

She felt remarkably like that damn cow in town who'd drawn too much attention.

"I wasn't stealing the car." They all stared at her, and the accusing look on Casey's face made her want to die. She wiped away tears and cleared her throat. "I left a note on the bed, explaining. I just wanted to get to town and I thought it'd probably be too far to walk. I would have left the car there for you to pick up."

Jordan frowned. "What'd you want in town that one of us couldn't get for you?"

"No, you don't understand. I was going to take the bus."

Morgan shook his head in a pitying way. "We don't have bus service in Buckhorn," he explained with little patience. "You'd have gotten to town and found it all closed up. Around here, they roll the sidewalks up at eight."

Her heart sank. "No bus service?"

Gabe pulled open the refrigerator and pulled out the milk. He drank straight from the carton. "The only bus service is in the neighboring county, a good forty miles away."

Honey watched him with a frown. "You shouldn't do that. It's not healthy."

Sawyer turned to glare down at her, his face filled with incredulous disbelief. She shrugged, feeling very small next to him. In a squeak, she said, "Well, it isn't."

Gabe finished the carton. "I knew it was almost empty."

"Oh."

Sawyer flexed his jaw. "What about your car? Your stuff? You don't even have any shoes, remember?"

He was still so furious, she took a step back. And even though Casey had looked wounded by what she'd attempted to do, he came to her side. He didn't say anything, just offered his silent support by standing close. She sent him a grateful smile, which he didn't return.

She shifted. "After I got things taken care of, I'd have sent for my stuff."

"Taken care of how?"

She'd known Sawyer was large, but now he seemed

even bigger, his anger exaggerating everything about him. There was no warmth in his dark eyes, no softness to his tone. She wasn't afraid of him, because she knew intuitively that he'd never hurt her. None of the brothers would hurt a woman; that type of contemptible behavior just wasn't in their genetic makeup. But she was terribly upset.

She opened her mouth, hoping to put him off until she wasn't quite so rattled, and he roared, *"No, God dammit, it will not wait until the morning!"*

She flinched. Silence filled the kitchen while she tried to decide how to react to his anger. Jordan stepped over to her, flanking her other side. "For God's sake, Sawyer, let her sit down. You're terrorizing her."

Sawyer's eyes narrowed and his jaw locked. With a vicious oath he turned away, then ran a hand through his dark hair. Just then Honey noticed Sawyer wore only boxers himself. Tight boxers. That hugged his muscled behind like a second skin.

Her lips parted. Her skin flushed. Blinking was an impossibility.

She stood there spellbound until Jordan set the cat down and started to lead her away. He held her arm with one hand and his sheet with the other and tried to take her to the table. Belatedly she realized his intent and held back because that would put her alongside Morgan, and she knew no one had thrown him any pants yet.

"I'm all right," she whispered, wishing Sawyer would look at her instead of staring out the window at the pitch black night.

Jordan released her with a worried frown. She went

back to the door and began picking up the keys and the contents of her purse. No one said anything, and when she was done, she carefully replaced the keys where they belonged. With her back to all of them, she said, "I wanted to get to the next town. I have a credit card, and I could charge a room, then call my sister to let her know I'm okay."

Jordan, Gabe and Morgan all asked, "You have a sister?" and, "Does she look like you?" and, "How old is she?"

Honey rolled her eyes. She couldn't believe they could be interested in that right now. "She's way prettier than me, but dark instead of fair, and she's a year younger. But the point is, she'll be worried. I told her I'd call her when I got settled somewhere. Then I'm going to hire a private detective to find out who's after me."

Casey frowned at her. "Why couldn't you do that from here?"

How could she tell him she was already starting to care too much about them all? Especially Sawyer? She tempered the truth and admitted, "I want to make things as simple as possible. I don't want to involve anyone else in my private problems."

Sawyer still hadn't turned or said a word, and it bothered her.

Gabe rooted through the cabinets for a cookie. "Why not just go to the police?"

She really hated to bare her soul, but it looked as if her time had run out. She clutched her purse tightly and stared at Sawyer's back. "My father is an influential man. Recently he decided to run for city council.

He's been campaigning, and things have looked promising so far. When I broke off my engagement, he was really angry because he'd planned to use the wedding as a means to campaign, inviting a lot of important, connected people to the normal round of celebrations that go with an engagement. Our relationship was already strained, and we'd barely spoken all week. He...well, he hit the roof when I told him I thought someone was after me. He thinks I'm just overreacting, letting my imagination run away because I'm distraught over the broken engagement. When I said I was going to the police, he threatened to cut me off because he says I'm causing him too much bad publicity, and he's certain I'll only make a fool of myself and draw a lot of unnecessary negative speculation that will damage his campaign."

Morgan started to stand, but when she squealed and covered her eyes, he sat back down again. "Casey, go get me something to wear, will you?"

"Why me? I don't wanna miss what's going on."

Morgan frowned at him. "I'm not dressed, that's why. And she's acting all squeamish about it, so she'd probably rather I didn't get up and parade around right now. Course, if you don't care how she feels..."

Put that way, Casey had little choice. He looked thoroughly disgruntled, and agreed with a lot of reluctance. "All right. But you owe me." He sauntered off, and the cat, apparently enjoying all the middle-of-the-night excitement, bounded after him.

Morgan folded his arms on the bar, looking like he'd made the most magnanimous gesture of all by offering to put on clothes. "So since your daddy threatened to cut the purse strings, you ran off instead?"

Now, that did it! It was almost one o'clock in the morning; she was tired, frazzled, embarrassed and worried. The last thing she intended to put up with was sarcasm.

Honey slammed her purse down on the counter and stalked over to face Morgan from the other side of the bar. Hands flat on the bar top, she leaned over until she was practically nose to nose with him. "Actually," she growled, forcing the words through her teeth, "I told him to stick his damn money where the sun doesn't shine."

Morgan pulled back, and astonishment flickered briefly in his cobalt eyes, mixed with a comical wariness. "Uh, you said that, did you?"

"Yes, I did. My father and I have never gotten along, and money won't change that."

Jordan applauded. "Good for you!"

She whipped about and pointed a commanding finger at Jordan. "You be quiet! All of you have done your best to bulldoze me, and I'm getting sick and tired of it. I don't take well to threats, and I couldn't care less about my father's money."

Jordan chuckled, not at all put off by her vehemence. "So what happened?"

Deflated by their eternal good humor, Honey sighed. Men in general were hard enough to understand, but these men were absolutely impossible. "He threatened to cut off my sister, instead, and though she reacted about the same as I did, I can't be responsible for that. I had no choice except to leave."

Sawyer spoke quietly from behind her. "Except that you got sick, so you didn't make it very far. At least, not far enough to feel safe."

She didn't turn to face him. Her gaze locked onto Gabe's, and he smiled in encouragement. As long as she didn't see the disappointment and resentment in Sawyer's eyes, she thought she'd be all right.

"Someone had been following me for two days. I wasn't imagining it. I know I wasn't." She spoke in the flattest monotone she could manage. She didn't want them to hear her fear, her worry. It left her feeling too exposed. "The first day I managed to dodge them."

"You say 'them.' Was there more than one person?"

She glanced at Morgan. "It's just a figure of speech. I never saw inside the car. It was a black Mustang, and the windows were darkened. I noticed it the day after I ended things with Alden. When I left the bank where I worked, the car was in the parking lot, and it followed me. I'd promised my sister to stop at the grocery, so I did, and it was there when I came out. It spooked me, so I drove around a little and managed to lose it by jumping on the expressway into the heavy traffic, then taking an exit that I never take."

Morgan rubbed his chin. "Must not have been a professional if you lost 'em that easy."

"I don't know if they're professional or not. I don't know anything about them."

Gabe leaned against the countertop, ankles crossed, eating cookies. "You know, I hate to say this, but you could have just been spooked. If that's all that happened—"

"That's not all! I'm not an idiot."

He held up both hands, one with a cookie in it, and mumbled, "I wasn't suggesting you are."

Totally ruffled, she glared at him a moment longer, then continued. "The car was there again the next day. And that's too much of a coincidence for me."

They each made various gestures of agreement, all but Sawyer, who merely continued to watch her through dark, narrowed eyes.

"This time it followed me right up until I pulled into my sister's house. The car slowed, waited, and I practically ran to get inside. Then it just drove away."

"I still think it's your ex," Jordan said. "If you left him, he probably wanted to know where you'd gone. I would have."

"Me, too," Gabe concurred.

"I thought it might be Alden at first. But it just doesn't fit." Honey watched Casey come back in with jeans and toss them to Morgan. Casual as you please, Morgan stood to put them on, and she quickly turned her back, but she could already feel the heat climbing up her neck to her cheeks. The man could improve with just an ounce of true modesty!

"So what changed your mind?"

Sawyer didn't look so angry now. Or rather, he didn't look so angry at *her*. He still seemed furious over the circumstances.

"I talked to Alden. He kicked up a fuss about me breaking things off, yelling about how humiliated he'd be since so many of his associates knew we were engaged. And he even threatened me some."

With cold fury, Sawyer whispered, "He threatened you?"

A chill went up her spine as she remembered again the lengths Alden had gone to just to punish her for breaking things off. And worst of all, she knew he wasn't motivated by love, but obviously by something much darker. "He used the same type of threats as my father. Alden told me he'd get me fired from my job, and he did. The bank claimed they were just scaling down employees, but Alden has a relative in a management position at the bank."

"You could sue," Jordan pointed out, and she saw he was now as angry as Sawyer. It was an unusual sight to see, since Jordan had always looked so serene. Now his green eyes were glittering with anger, his lean jaw locked.

"I...I might have," she admitted, dumbfounded by their support, "but that night when I was at my sister's house, someone broke in. She was out on a late date, so I was alone. I could hear them going through the drawers, the cabinets. I *know* it was the same people who'd been following me. They saw where I was staying and then they came back. They went through everything. I just don't know why, or what they were looking for. I'm ashamed to admit it, but I don't think I've ever been so afraid in my life. For the longest time I couldn't move. I just laid in the bed, frozen, listening. When I realized they'd eventually search the bedroom, I forced myself to get up. I didn't bother getting clothes, I just grabbed up my purse, slipped out the bedroom window and snuck to my car. I saw the curtain open in the front room as I started the engine, then I just concentrated on getting away. I was nearly hysterical by the time I got to my father's."

She lowered her face, embarrassed and shaken all over again. Masculine hands touched her, patting her back, stroking her head, and gruff words of comfort were murmured. She was caught between wanting to laugh and wanting to cry.

She pulled herself together and lifted her chin. After a deep breath, she continued, and the men all subsided back to their original lounging posts.

"My father took me seriously this time, at least for awhile. He sent some men over to check out the apartment, but they said nothing seemed to be out of place. The only thing open was the window I'd gone through, and there was no one there when they arrived. Again, my father thought I was just overreacting. He wanted to call Alden, thinking I'd feel better when we got back together."

Sawyer never said a word, but Morgan grunted. "Did you tell him the bastard had cost you your job?"

She shrugged. "My father said he was just acting out of wounded male pride."

"Hogwash." Gabe tossed the rest of the cookies aside to pace around the kitchen. Though he wore only his underwear, he made an awesome sight. "Men don't threaten women, period."

"That's what my sister said. My father had sent men to get her, also, before he decided there wasn't a problem, that I'd made it all up. Luckily she believed me. She promised not to go back to the house until after a security alarm was put in—a concession from my father, which my sister refused, saying she'd get her own."

Jordan grinned. "Your sister sounds a lot like you."

Why that amused him, she couldn't guess. "In some ways."

Gabe looked thoroughly disgusted. "Someone is following you around town, looting through your house with you in it, and the best your father could do was offer an alarm system?"

Honey held up her hands. She couldn't very well explain her father's detachment when the very idea would be alien to such protective men. Why, even now, they'd gathered in the kitchen, in the middle of the night, pulled from their beds, and no one was complaining. They just wanted to help.

Those damn tears welled in her eyes again.

Morgan flexed his knuckles, and the look on his face was terrifying. Even though she felt disturbed rehashing the whole story, Honey smiled. They were all so overprotective, so wonderful. She couldn't drag them into her mess. She had no idea how much danger she might actually be in. "When I left my father's that afternoon, the car was there again, following me, and I *did* panic. I took off. But it followed, and even tried to run me off the road."

Jordan stared at her. "Good God."

"It kept coming alongside me, and when I wouldn't pull over, it...it hit the back of my car. The first time, I managed to keep control, but then it happened again, and the third time I went into a spin. The Mustang had to hit his brakes, too, to keep from barreling into me, and there was an oncoming car and the Mustang lost control. He went off the side of the road and crashed into a guardrail. The other car stopped to see if he was hurt, but I just kept going."

"And you've been going ever since?"

She nodded. "I left Alden a week ago. It seems like a year. I stopped once and traded in my car, which was a nice little cherry-red Chevy Malibu, not worth much with the recent damage in the back. I bought that old rusted Buick instead. But I've been so on edge. I stopped to get gas once, and saw the Mustang again. I have no doubt I'm being followed, I just don't know why. Alden didn't really care about me, so it seems insane he'd go to this much trouble to harass me. And harassing me certainly wouldn't make me reconsider marrying him."

Sawyer pulled out a kitchen chair then forced her to sit in it. He said to Jordan, "Why don't you put on some coffee or something? Casey, you should go on back to bed."

Casey, who'd been sitting at the table, his head in his hand, looking weary, said, "No way."

"Chores still have to be done tomorrow."

"I'll manage."

Honey, relieved to be off her feet, smiled at him. "Really, Casey. You should get some sleep. There's not anything else to hear tonight, anyway."

Sawyer crouched down beside her, his expression intent, his nearness overpowering. She couldn't be this close to him without wanting to touch him, to get closer still. And right now, he had all that warm, male skin exposed. She turned her face away, but he brought it back with a touch on her chin. "Now there's where you're wrong, sweetheart. You're going to tell me why you agreed to marry this bastard in the first place, and why he wanted to marry you. Then you're going to tell me what made you change your mind. And if we have to sit here all night to get the full truth, then that's what we'll do."

She knew she'd get no rest until he had his way, and she was limp from the nerve-racking experience of trying to steal away and getting caught in the act. She folded her hands primly in her lap and nodded. "Very well. But at least get dressed." She looked over her shoulder at the others. "*All* of you. If I'm to be forced through the inquisition, I demand at least that much respect."

Sawyer stared at her hard, and she couldn't tell if it was amusement, annoyance or sexual awareness that brought on that hardness to his features. His gaze skimmed over her, then lit on her face. "Fair enough. But Casey will stay here to keep an eye on you. Don't even think about running off again."

He walked away, and she admitted she'd been wrong on all accounts. It was distrust that had been so evident on his face. And she had to admit she'd deserved it.

8

WHEN SAWYER STALKED into his room to grab some pants, still angry and doubly frustrated, the first thing he saw was the rumpled bed where she'd lain. Heat drifted over him in waves, making his vision hazy. He wanted her so badly he shook with it, and he knew the wanting wouldn't go away. He hadn't even known that kind of lust existed, because it never had for him before. Unlike Morgan, and even Gabe, he'd always had a handle on his sexuality. He was, more often than not, cool and remote, and *always* in control.

And after the way his wife had played him, used him, after suffering such a huge disappointment, he'd made a pact never to get involved again. Yet he'd been involved with Honey from the second he'd seen her in the car. He'd lifted her out, and awareness had sizzled along his nerve endings. He wanted to rail against the truth of that, but knew it wouldn't do him any good. When he'd caught her stealing keys from the kitchen, his only thought was that she was leaving, not about the damn car, not about the danger she'd be in.

He hadn't wanted her to go.

He needed to get her out of his system so he could function normally again, instead of teetering between one extreme reaction and another. He didn't like it. He wanted his calm reserve back. But how?

And then he saw the note and remembered. She'd written a note to explain why she felt it necessary to sneak away from him. His fists clenched, and every muscle pulled taut as he struggled with his fierce temper—a temper he hadn't even known he had until he'd met Miss Honey Malone. Damn, but it filled him with rage. She didn't trust him at all, on any level. Curiosity and resentment exploded inside him, and he took two long strides to the mattress and snatched up the sealed envelope. His name was written across the front in a very feminine scrawl. He started to tear it open, but caught himself in time and carefully loosened the seal instead.

She'd written on a cash receipt, probably the only paper she could find on his dresser. All stationery was kept in his office. He drew a deep breath, ready to witness her lame excuses for trying to sneak out—and what he read instead made his knees buckle. He dropped heavily to the side of the bed as his heart raced.

Sawyer,
I know you won't be happy that I'm leaving this way, but it's for the best. I'm finding I want you too much to stay. Since you made it clear you'd rather not get involved, and I know it wouldn't be wise anyway, I have to leave. I can't trust myself around you.

His eyes widened as he read the words, amazed that she'd written them and even more so that she'd had the audacity to put a smily face there, as well, as if poking fun at herself and her lack of restraint around him. The little drawing looked teasing and playful and made him hard as a stone. She wanted him? And she thought he should be amused by that?

He swallowed hard and finished the note.

To be honest, you're just too tempting. Shameful of me to admit, but it's true. And I'm afraid I'm not sure how to deal with it, since I've never had to before. I hope you understand.

Please forgive me for taking your car. I'll leave it at the bus station with the keys inside, so bring a spare set to open it. When I get things resolved, I swear I'll send you a check to pay for the damage to your fence, and your incredible hospitality. I won't ever forget you,

Honey

He wanted to go grab her and put her over his knee, not only because she would have risked herself in what he now realized was very real danger, but because she'd have been leaving for all the wrong reasons. And she'd offered him a check. He wanted to howl. He didn't want her money and he never had. How many times did he have to tell her that?

Morgan tapped on the door and stuck his head inside. "You found the note?"

Sawyer quickly folded it. Since he hadn't put pants on yet he had nowhere to put it. "Yeah. It, uh, it said she'd leave the car at the bus station with the keys locked inside, just like she told us."

Morgan crossed his arms and leaned against the

door frame. He still wore only jeans, but he had at least put the gun away. "I don't suppose you'd let me see the note?"

"Why?"

"Idle curiosity?"

Sawyer grunted. "Yeah, right. More like plain old nosiness." Sawyer kept his back to his brother, more than a little aware of how obvious his erection was at this point.

His gaze met Morgan's in the mirror over the dresser, and he saw Morgan was struggling to contain his grin. "I gather you got something to hide there?"

Opening a drawer and pulling out a casual pair of khakis, Sawyer mumbled negligently, "Don't know why you'd think that."

"The way you're clutching that note? And acting so secretive and protective?" He laughed. "Don't worry. I won't say a word. Take your time getting dressed. I think I'll just go round up something to eat."

"Morgan?"

"Yeah?"

"Don't mention to her that I have the note."

"Whatever you say, Sawyer." Then he laughed again and walked away.

After carefully easing his zipper up and buttoning his slacks, Sawyer smoothed out the note, removing the wrinkles caused by his fist. He neatly folded it and slid it into his back pocket, making certain it was tucked completely out of sight. He'd talk to her about the note—hell, yes, he had a lot to say about it—but that could be taken care of after everything else was straightened out.

He didn't bother with a shirt or shoes, and when he entered the kitchen, he saw the rest of the men had felt the same. Gabe had on shorts; Morgan and Jordan wore jeans.

Honey was at the stove cooking.

His every instinct sharpened at the sight of her. She, too, was barefoot, her hair now pulled back in a long, sleek ponytail that swished right above her pert behind—a smooth, very soft behind he'd stroked with his palms. As he drank in the sight of her with new admiration, he felt like a predator, ready to close in. With that tell-all note, she'd sealed her own fate. He wanted her, and now that he knew she wanted him, too, he'd have her; he wasn't noble enough to do otherwise. After the other issues were resolved, he'd explain to her one more time how he felt about commitment, and then they'd deal with the personal issue of lust.

He glanced at his brothers who sat around the table like a platoon waiting to be fed, and he frowned. They shrugged back, each wearing a comical face of helplessness. Sawyer growled a curse and stepped up to Honey. "What the hell are you doing?"

Without raising her head, she barked back, "Cooking."

His brows lifted. He heard one of the brothers snicker. Crossing his arms over his naked chest, he said, "You wanna tell me why?"

She whirled, a hot spatula in her hand, which she pointed at his chest, forcing him to take a hasty step back. "Because I'm hungry. And because they're hungry!" The spatula swung wildly to encompass the men, who quickly nodded in agreement to her fierce look.

"And I'm tired of being coddled and treated like I'm helpless. You want me to stay, fine. I'll stay. But I'll be damned if I'm going to lay around and be waited on and feel like I owe the lot of you."

Sawyer leaned away from the blast of her anger, totally bowled over by this new temperament. Cautiously, he took another step back. "No one wants you to feel beholden."

"Well, I *do!*"

"Okay, okay." He tried to soothe her and got a dirty look for his efforts. "You want to cook, fine," he added with a calm he didn't feel.

"Ha! I wasn't asking your permission. And don't try that placating tone on me because Jordan already did. And he's much better at it than you are."

He glanced at his brother, only to see Jordan's ears turn red. She was intimidating his brothers! Sawyer crowded close again and opened his mouth, only to meet that spatula once more.

"And don't try bullying me, because Morgan has been at it since I met him, and I'm not putting up with it anymore. Do you know he told me I wasn't allowed to cook because I was sick? He tried to force me to sit down. Well, I'll sit down when I'm good and ready. Not before."

Sawyer had no idea what had set her off this time, but he almost grinned, anxious to find out. Now that he'd decided against denying himself, he wanted to absorb her every nuance instead of fighting against her allure.

"Am I allowed to ask what you're cooking, or will you threaten me with that spatula again?"

She tilted her head, saw he wasn't going to argue with her and nodded. "Grilled ham and cheese. Do you know Gabe was about to give that box of cookies to Casey? Or at least, the ones he hadn't already eaten. If we're going to do this interrogation, we might as well eat properly rather than shoving sugar down our throats."

Sawyer looked at Gabe in time to see him sneak a cookie from his lap and pop it into his mouth. He laughed out loud.

"You think that's funny? And here you are a doctor. You should be telling them about healthy diets and all that."

"Honey, have you looked at my brothers? They're all pretty damn physically fit."

She tucked her chin in, and a delicate flush rose on her cheeks. "Yeah, well, I noticed, but Casey is still a growing boy. He should eat better." She put another sandwich on a plate, and it was only then Sawyer noticed there were six plates, meaning she'd made one for him, too. The sandwiches were neatly cut, and there were pickle slices and carrot curls beside them. He honestly didn't think any of his brothers had ever in their lives eaten carrot curls.

She'd turned the coffeepot off and poured glasses of milk instead. Sawyer started carrying plates to the table, since his brothers had evidently been ordered to sit, given that none of them were moving much. They all looked uncomfortable, but then, they weren't used to getting waited on. Their mother hadn't been the type to mollycoddle once they'd all gotten taller than her, which had happened at the tail end of grade school.

"Casey gets more physical exercise than most grown men. And he gets a good variety of things to eat. My mother harped on that plenty when he was first born."

Casey grinned. "And they're all still at it. I get measured almost daily to make sure I'm still growing like I should be, and because Grandma calls and checks. She says the good part is, they all eat more vegetables and fruits because they keep the stuff around for me."

Honey looked slightly mollified by their explanations. Sawyer held her chair out for her, and as she sat, he smoothed his palm down the tail of her hair, letting his fingers trail all the way to the base of her spine, where they lingered for a heartbeat. He imagined her incredible hair, so silky and cool, loose over his naked body as she rode him, his hands clamped on her hips to hold her firm against him. A rush of primal recognition made his breath catch. He wanted to pick her up from the table and carry her off to his room.

Of course he wouldn't do that, so he ignored the startled look she gave him and forced himself to step away.

Everyone waited until she'd taken her first bite, then they dug in with heartfelt groans of savory appreciation. It *was* good, Sawyer had to admit, even the damn carrot curls.

Sitting directly across from her, he couldn't help but watch as Honey took a small bite of her own sandwich. His thoughts wandered again to the note. *She wanted him.* He forgot to chew as he watched her slender fingers pick up a sliver of carrot, watched her soft lips close around it. He saw her lashes lower, saw soft wisps of blond hair fall over her temple.

Gabe nudged him, and he choked.

"I don't mean to drag you from whatever ruminations you were mired in, but don't you want to ask her some questions? I mean, that is why we're all up at two in the morning, gathered around the table eating instead of sleeping, right?"

Sawyer drank half his milk to wash down the bite of sandwich and nodded. "Come on, Honey. 'Fess up."

She sent him a fractious glare, but she did pat her mouth with her napkin, then folded her hands primly as if preparing to be a sacrifice. She didn't look at anyone in particular, but neither did she lower her face. She stared between him and Gabe, her chin lifted, her shoulders squared.

"I found out my fiancé had only asked to marry me to inherit my father's assets. All his stock, his company, the family home, is willed to my future husband, whoever the man might be."

There was a shock of silence as they all tried to comprehend such a mercenary act, but Sawyer was more tuned to her features. This was such a blow to her pride; he saw that now. He shouldn't have forced this confrontation, certainly not in front of everyone.

"Honey..."

"It doesn't matter." She still hadn't looked at him. Her fingers nervously pleated her napkin, but her chin stayed high. "My father and I never got along. I love him, but I don't like him much. I think he feels the same way about me. He's always resented having daughters instead of sons." Her gaze touched on each of them, and she gave a small smile. "He'd love the lot of you, a household full of big, capable men. But my sister and I never quite measured up."

"I have to tell you, I don't like your father much."

She laughed at Jordan. "Yeah, well, he's had hell putting up with me. We've butted heads since I was sixteen. When I refused to get involved in the business, which is basically electronics, new computer hardware and very state-of-the-art sort of things, he cut me out of his will. I knew it, but I didn't care. What I didn't know is that he'd changed the will to benefit the man I'd someday marry." Her mouth tightened and her eyes flickered away. Then in a whisper, she finished. "When Alden started pursuing me, I thought it was because he cared. Not because he had discovered my father's intentions."

There was, of course, the natural barrage of questions. Sawyer got up and moved to sit beside her but remained silent, letting his brothers do the interrogating. He no longer had the heart for it. He picked up her cold hand from her lap and cradled it between his own. She clutched at him, squeezing his fingers tight, but otherwise made no sign of even noticing his touch.

Gently, Gabe asked, "Why didn't you want to be in your father's business?"

She answered without hesitation. "It's a cutthroat environment. Company spies, takeovers, social climbers. It kept my father away from home the entire time my sister and I were growing up. I hate the business. I'd never involve myself in it. I wasn't even keen on marrying a man who worked for my father. But Alden led me to believe he was content with the position of regional manager, that he didn't aspire to anything more. It seemed…like a good idea."

She blushed making that admission, and Sawyer rubbed his thumb over her knuckles to comfort her. "Because your father approved of Alden?"

"Yes." She looked shamed, and he almost pulled her into his lap, then her shoulders stiffened and he saw her gather herself. In many ways, he was as drawn by her spirit and pride as he was by the sexual chemistry that shimmered between them.

She sighed. "I hadn't realized I was still trying to gain my father's approval. But then I went to see Alden at the office, to discuss some of the wedding plans, and his secretary was out to lunch. I heard him talking on the phone about his new status once the marriage was final. I listened just long enough to find out he was making grand plans, all because marrying me would put him in a better social and professional position. It hit me that I was angry and embarrassed over being so stupid, but I wasn't…I wasn't lovesick over learning the truth. In fact, I was sort of relieved to have a good reason to break things off, strange as that may sound. So I went back to his house, packed and left him the note."

Morgan rubbed his chin. "Company status seems like a pretty good reason for him to want you back, to possibly be following you."

She shrugged. "But why try to hurt me? Why try to run me off the road? Without me, there'd be no marriage and then he'd gain nothing. And when my sister's house was broken into, what were they looking for? That's what doesn't make sense. Alden is already in a good financial position. And as my father's regional manager, he's on his way to the top of the company. It's not like he *needed* to marry me to get anywhere. All that would accomplish was to speed things along."

"Maybe." Morgan finished his last carrot curl, then got up to fetch a pencil and paper. "I want you to write down your father's name, the company name, addresses for both and for this Alden ass, and anything else you can think of. I'll check on some things in the morning." He hushed her before she could speak. "Discreetly. I promise. No one will follow you here from anything I say or do."

She tugged on Sawyer's hand, and he released her so she could write. Gabe stood up with a yawn. "I'll start work on your car tomorrow, as long as you promise you won't go anywhere without telling one of us first."

Absently, she nodded, her attention on making her list for Morgan.

"Good. Then I'm off to bed. Come on, Casey. You look like you're ready to collapse under the table."

Casey grinned tiredly, but rather than leave, he walked around the table and gave Honey a brief kiss on the forehead. She looked up, appearing both startled and pleased by the gesture.

Casey smiled down at her. "Thanks for the sandwich. It was way better than cookies."

Morgan gently clasped the back of her neck when he took the note from her. "I can see why you've been cautious, but that's over now, right?"

When she didn't agree quickly enough, he wobbled her head. "Right?"

She gave him a disgruntled frown. "Yes."

"Good girl. I'll see you in the morning. Saywer, you should hit the sack, too. You got almost no sleep the night before, and you're starting to look like a zombie."

Sawyer waved him off. He was anxious for everyone to get the hell out of the room. He had a few things he wanted to say to Honey that would be better said in private.

Jordan pulled her out of her chair for a hug. "Sleep tight, Honey. And no more worrying. Everything will be okay now. Sawyer will take good care of you."

She glanced at Sawyer, then quickly away. He wondered if his intentions showed on his face, given the timid way she avoided looking right at him. He didn't doubt it was possible. He felt like a sexual powder keg with a very short fuse.

Finally they were alone in the kitchen. Honey gathered up the plates and carried them to the dishwasher, her movements unnaturally jerky and nervous. Sawyer watched her through hot eyes, tracking her as she came back to the table for the glasses.

"You're feeling better?"

"Yes." She deftly loaded the dishwasher, as much to keep from looking at him as anything else. He could feel her reservations, her uncertainty. He stepped close enough to inhale her spicy scent, leaning down so his nose almost touched her nape, exposed by the way she'd tied her hair back. She stilled, resting her hands on the edge of the counter. She kept her back to him, and when she spoke, her voice was breathy. "My...my throat is still a little sore, but I don't feel so wrung out. I think all the sleep helped."

He crowded closer still and placed his hands beside hers, caging her in. Deliberately he allowed his chest to press against her shoulder blades. "I have patients in the morning, but in the afternoon I'll take you into town to get a few things."

"Things?"

"Whatever you might need." He nuzzled the soft skin beneath her ear. "More clothes, definitely shoes." His mouth touched her earlobe. "Anything you want."

"I'll pay for it myself."

"Not unless you have cash. Your credit cards can be traced." He kissed her skin softly, then added, "We can call it a brief loan if that'll make you feel better." He had no intention of letting her pay him back, but she didn't need to know that now. Fighting with her was the absolute last thing on his mind.

Her head fell forward. "All right."

He pulled his hands slowly from the counter, letting them trail up her arms to her sides, then down and around to her belly. He heard her suck in a quick, startled breath. His body throbbed; he nestled his erection against her soft behind, finding some comfort from the razor edge of arousal and intensifying the ache at the same time. His fingers kneaded her soft, flat belly, and when she moaned, he trailed one hand higher to her breast, free beneath the smooth cotton of the T-shirt.

Just as she'd done the last time he'd touched her there, she jerked violently, as if the mere press of his fingers was both an acute pleasure and an electrifying pain. His heart thundered at the feel of her soft weight in his hand. Her nipple was already peaked, burning against his palm. She'd instinctively pulled backward from the touch of his hand, and now she was pressed hard against him.

He adjusted his hold, one hand clamping on her breast, the other opened wide over her abdomen. In a growled whisper, he said, "I read your note."

As he'd expected, she exploded into motion, trying to get away. He held her secure with his firm hold and said, "Shh. Shh, it's all right."

She sounded panicked. "I...I'd forgotten!"

"I know." He didn't release her, adjusting his hold to keep her still, to keep her right where he wanted her. "I should let you sleep. I should give you time to think about this. But I want you too much. Now."

He could feel her trembling, the rapid hammering of her heart. He turned his hand slightly until his thumb could drag over her sensitive nipple, flicking once, twice. Her hands gripped the countertop hard, and she panted.

Opening his mouth on her throat, he sucked the delicate skin against his teeth. He wanted to mark her; he wanted to devour her. The primitive urges were new to him, but he no longer fought against them. She was his now, and there was no going back.

He caught her nipple between his rough fingertips and plucked gently. She moaned, then gave a soft sob, and all the resistance left her until she stood limp and trembling against him.

"You want me, Honey."

Her head moved on his shoulder, and her voice was faint with excitement. "Yes. That's why I had to leave. It's...too soon, but I was so disappointed when you said you didn't want me. I knew I couldn't trust myself...."

He pressed his erection hard against her and wondered what it would be like to take her this way, from behind, her plump breasts filling his hands, her legs quivering....

"It's only sex, sweetheart. That's all I can give you." The words emerged as a rough growl because he didn't want to say them, didn't want to take the chance she'd turn him away. But from somewhere deep inside himself, his honor had forced him to admit the truth to her.

To his surprise, she merely nodded, then repeated, "Only sex. That's probably for the best."

A surprising wash of indignation hit him, even as he admitted to himself the reaction was totally unfair. She'd only agreed with him, yet he'd thought she felt more. *He did.* Whether or not he admitted it, he knew it was true, and he hated it. He couldn't get involved. Never again.

He turned her around, then lifted her in his arms. "So be it. At least we're agreed."

She clutched at his shoulders and stared up at him with wide eyes. "What are you doing?"

He was burning up with urgent need, making his pace too rushed. He wanted to take his time with her, but as he looked down at her, seeing the same shimmering heat in her gaze, he wondered if he'd even make it to his room. It seemed much too far away.

"Sawyer?"

Her voice shook, and he bent to place a hard, quick

kiss to her soft mouth. "I'm taking you to bed. Then I'm going to strip you naked and make love to you."

That sexy mouth of hers parted and she gasped. "But... It's late."

The bedroom door was already open and he walked in, then quietly shoved it closed with his heel. "If you think I'm going to wait one second more, especially after reading that note, you're dead wrong." He lowered her to the mattress, but followed her down, unwilling to have any space between them at all. In one movement he used his knee to open her slender thighs and settled between her legs. He wanted to groan aloud at the exquisite contact, at the feel of her soft body cushioning his. Damn, if he wasn't careful, he'd come before he ever got inside her.

He cupped her face to make certain he had her attention. "If you'd gotten away today, I'd have come after you." Her eyes turned dark, her pupils expanding with awareness. "There's something between us, and damned if I can fight it anymore. I don't think I could stand going the rest of my life without knowing what it'd be like to have you under me, naked, mine."

She stared up at him, her breathing fast and low, then with a moan she lifted while at the same time pulling him down. Their mouths met, open, hot, and Sawyer gave up any hopes of slowing down. He'd only known her a few short days, but he felt like he'd been waiting on her for a lifetime.

9

SHE WAS ALIVE with sensation, aware of Sawyer on every possible level, the hardness of his body, his heat, the way his kiss had turned commanding, his tongue thrusting deep into her mouth, stroking. She breathed in his hot, musky, male scent, felt the rasp of a slight beard stubble, and she moaned hungrily. Every touch, every movement, drove her closer to the brink. She'd never experienced this flash fire of desire before and probably would have argued over its existence. But now she was held on the very threshold of exploding, and all he'd done was kiss her.

Her hands moved over his bare back, loving the feel of hot flesh and hard muscle. She'd seen more male perfection in the past two days than most women experienced in a lifetime, but nothing and no one could compare to the man now making love to her. Desperately, she pulled her mouth free and groaned out a plea. *"Sawyer..."*

It seemed to be happening too fast. Her body was taut, her breasts swollen and acutely sensitive. And where his pelvis pushed against her, she ached unbearably.

"It's all right," he whispered against her mouth, the words rushed and low. "Let me get this shirt off you."

Before he'd finished speaking, the T-shirt was

tugged above her breasts. He paused, staring down at her with black eyes, and one large hand covered her right breast. His fingertips were caloused, and they rasped over her puckered nipple, around it, pinching lightly. She cried out, her body arching hard. The pleasure was piercing, sharp, pulling her deeper. He soothed her with mumbled words, then bent, and his mouth replaced his hand.

With a gasp, her eyes opened wide. She couldn't bear it. His mouth was so hot, his tongue rough, and then he started sucking. Hard. All the while his hips moved in that tantalizing rhythm against her in a parody of what was to come. She lost her fragile grasp on control, unaware of everything but the implosion of heat, the wave of sensation that made her muscles ripple and her skin burn, the link between her breasts and her groin and the way he touched her, how he moved against her...

Without thought, she dug her nails into his bare shoulders and she tightened her thighs around his hard hips, sinking her teeth into her bottom lip and groaning long and low with the intensity of her orgasm.

After a moment the feelings began to subside, leaving her shaken and confused. Sawyer raised his head, his lips wet, his eyes blazing. He stared at her and whispered, "Damn."

She shared his sentiments. Shock mingled with sated desire. She hadn't even known such a thing was possible, much less that it would ever happen to her. She wasn't, in the normal course of things, an overly sexual woman, and gaining her own pleasure had always been an elusive thing, not a bombarding rush.

He kissed her gently, and all she could do was struggle for breath, unable to even pucker for his kiss. His hand trembled as he smoothed hair away from her face, now pulled loose from the string she'd tied it back with. "I didn't expect that," he admitted, still softly, with awe.

She swallowed hard, trying to gain her bearings. A pleasurable throb reverberated through her limp muscles. She could barely think. "Wh...what?"

He touched her cheek and a gentle smile lit up his face. Without a word, he sat up astride her thighs and pulled the T-shirt the rest of the way off, lifting each arm as if she were a child. "You are so damn sweet."

She covered her aching breasts with her hands, shyness over what had just happened engulfing her. Sawyer ignored the gesture as he looked at her body with an absorption that left her squirming. His hands smoothed over her shoulders, down her sides. He touched her navel with his baby finger, dipping lightly, then flicking open the snap to her jeans.

"I want you naked. I want to look my fill."

What he said and the heat in his words made her entire body blush. He smiled, then moved to the side of her to wrest her jeans down her legs. "Lift your hips."

She swallowed her embarrassment and did as he asked, anxious to see what would come next. So far, nothing had been as she'd anticipated, or what she'd come to expect between men and women. Then he took her panties with her jeans, and as he looked at the curls between her legs, she squeezed her eyes shut.

They snapped open again when the bed dipped and she felt his mouth gently brush over the top of one thigh. "Sawyer!"

He reversed the position of his upper body so that he faced the foot of the bed; his arms caged her hips and again he kissed her, this time flicking his tongue out and tasting her skin. "Open your legs for me," he growled low.

She released her breasts to clutch at the sheet, trying to ground herself against the unbearable eroticism of his command. He didn't hurry her, didn't repeat his order. He merely waited and finally, after two deep breaths, she found the courage to do as he asked. She felt stiff with expectation and nervousness and excitement as she felt herself slowly exposed.

He made a low rasping sound of appreciation, then whispered, "Wider."

Shaking from head to toe, she bent one knee, and with a raw groan, he took swift advantage. She felt his hot moist breath, the touch of his lips on the inside of her thigh, then higher, until he was there, kissing her, nuzzling into her femininity. With a jolt of red hot lust, she lifted her hips, the movement involuntary and instinctive, offering herself to him completely.

"Easy, sweetheart." His hands slid under her, locking around her thighs, keeping her still. Keeping her wide open.

She felt the bold stroke of his tongue, then the seeking press of his lips before he found what he wanted and treated her to another, more gentle but twice as devastating suckle.

She was sensitive and swollen from her recent climax, and the feel of his mouth there was both a relief and a wild torment. She had a single moment of cognizance and pulled a pillow over her head to muffle her raw cries, and then she was climaxing again. And again. Sawyer reveled in her reactions, and she found he could be totally ruthless when he chose to be. He used his fingers, gently manipulating her. He used his tongue to make her beg, his teeth to make her gasp. And she gladly obeyed.

When he stood by the side of the bed, she no longer tried to cover herself. She doubted she could move. Her legs were still sprawled, her breasts trembling with her low, shallow breaths, but she didn't care. She felt replete and wrung out and willingly pliant.

Sawyer shucked off his jeans, his face dark with desire, his breathing labored. Honey let her head fall to the side so she could see him better, and through narrowed, slumberous eyes, she took in the gorgeous sight of his naked body. Though she didn't move, her heart gave a heavy thump at the sight he presented.

His shoulders and chest were wide, his stomach hard, his thighs long and muscled. The hair around his groin was darker, and his erection was long and thick, pulsing in impatience. She shuddered at the sight of it, wondering if she could bear taking him inside when everything else he'd done had already shattered her. She felt emotionally raw, unable to cope with the depth of what she'd experienced, of what he could so easily make her feel.

She watched as he opened the nightstand drawer and pulled out a slim pack of condoms. He tore one open and deftly slid it on, then turned to stare down at her.

She whispered, "I didn't know, didn't think..." but she couldn't put into words the way he'd made her feel, how it both thrilled and alarmed her. She could tell by the grim set of his features he understood, and to some degree, felt the same. They both resented the strength of the desire between them. Mere sex shouldn't be so consuming, so uncontrollable.

"I can feel you everywhere," she added in the same low tone, almost fearfully because she'd never suspected sex could be so wild and forceful, to the point she was helpless against it. Her skin still tingled, her senses alive though her body was sated.

Remaining at the side of the bed, his eyes hot on her face, Sawyer reached down and cupped his hand over her sex. His fingers moved gently between her slick folds until they opened; he pressed his middle finger inside her, and his eyes closed on a groan. "Damn, you're wet and tight."

Honey bit her lip and tears seeped from the corners of her eyes as she struggled to accept this new onslaught of sensation. "It's...it's too much, Sawyer."

"And not enough," he rasped, then came into the bed over her.

She opened herself to him without reserve, lifting her face for his kiss. Though the hunger was still tightly etched in his features, his kiss was gently controlling. He took his time, making love to her mouth, bringing her desire back into full swing.

"Please."

Sawyer cupped her face and stared into her eyes.

"Wrap your legs high around my waist. That's it. Now hold me tight."

His voice was so low and gruff she could barely understand him. She felt him probing, his erection pressing just inside, burning and appeasing, and her heart swelled. She gave a shuddering sob and closed her eyes, but he kissed her and said, "Look at me, Honey."

It was so wonderful, it hurt. She cried while she stared at him, not out of sadness, but from inexplicable pleasure. She knew she'd probably fallen in love within the first hour of meeting him. She drew her palms down his chest to his small brown nipples and smoothed over them, determined to take everything she could. His expression hardened and he locked his jaw, rocking against her, entering her by excruciatingly slow degrees. She lifted her hips to hurry him along and was rewarded with his harsh groan. His muscles rippled and tightened, and then he thrust hard with a curse.

Honey held on to him, stunned by the shock of pleasure as he filled her. He tangled his fingers in her hair and locked his mouth onto hers and rode her hard. His chest rubbed against her stiffened nipples, his hips grinding into her with an incredible friction, his scent invading her.

She screamed as she climaxed, and Sawyer, still kissing her, swallowed the sound. He held her so close she felt a part of him. He held her and kissed her until she'd relaxed and then continued doing so even as he found his own release, his hold almost crushing it became so tight.

The kiss dwindled, turning light and soft and lazy as

Sawyer sank onto her. His heartbeat rocked them both, and still he kept kissing her, easily, consuming her, soft lazy kisses that went on and on.

A noise in the hallway made him lift his head. He stared toward the closed door, and Honey couldn't remember if he'd locked it or not. After a second of squeaking floorboards, she heard Morgan call softly, "Sawyer?"

Sawyer dropped his forehead onto hers with a muffled curse. He swallowed, took two deep breaths and said with feigned calm, "Yeah?"

"Ah, I heard a scream. Again. But I'll assume you're...kissing her again." There was a slight chuckle. "Carry on." Then the sound of retreating footsteps.

Honey wanted to cover her face; she even wanted to blush. She couldn't manage either one. She closed her eyes and started to drift off to sleep. Sawyer kissed her slack mouth, smoothed his rough hand over her cheek, then rolled to her side. He was silent for a few minutes, and she felt the weight of lethargy settle into her bones. Right before she dozed off, she heard him murmur, "God knows I got more than I bargained for, but I intend to keep taking it while you're here."

And how long would that be, she wondered? Two days, maybe three? With Gabe fixing her car and Morgan checking into things, she wouldn't have much time at all. But like Sawyer, she intended to make every minute count.

In the next instant, she was sound asleep.

SAWYER WATCHED HONEY with a brooding intensity. She'd been here two weeks now, and he'd made love to her at least twice a day. Yet it wasn't enough, and he'd begun to doubt there could ever be enough. She wasn't out of his system—far from it. It seemed the more he had her, the more he wanted her, to the point he could think of little else.

She'd integrated herself completely into their lives. She now took turns cooking and cleaning, regardless of how they all complained. Unlike the other women who on rare occasions had visited the house, Honey didn't suggest they should sit and let her do it all. She didn't excuse them from duty just because they were male. No, she willingly allowed them their fair share. But she wanted to do her own part, too.

Seeing her in his kitchen cooking made him want her.

Seeing her pulling weeds from the flower beds around the house made him want her.

And listening to her argue with his brothers or coddle his son really made him burn with lust. Dammit. This wasn't the way it was supposed to be.

It was late in the day, and a barrage of patients had kept him busy for several solid hours. He hadn't had a chance to visit with her as he usually did. Twice she had poked her head into his office to offer him lunch or a quick snack. Even seeing her for those brief moments had brightened his day, as if he'd grown accustomed to her and had been suffering withdrawal from her absence.

He didn't like the feeling. Never before had he felt annoyed by having so many patients, or having to deal with the occasional imaginary illness. He was known for his patience and kindness, not his lust.

But lust today had ruled him, just as it had since he'd first laid eyes on her.

Right now, Honey was hanging over Gabe's shoulder while he looked at her car engine. Gabe had done a fair job of taking his time on the car. He'd ordered unnecessary parts, replaced things that didn't need replacing and generally stalled as long as he could. But Honey was getting antsy. There'd been no sign of the men after her, and Morgan hadn't been able to turn up a damn thing, though he'd alerted several people in town to let him know of any strangers passing through. Now all they could do was wait, but Honey was done waiting. She'd gotten it into her head that she was taking advantage of them and therefore should get out from underfoot.

Sawyer grunted to himself as he leaned on the shed door, watching her and Gabe together. His hair was still wet from his recent shower, but the heat pounding down on his head and radiating from the lush ground would quickly dry it. Already his T-shirt was starting to stick to his back, and his temper felt precarious at best, in sync with the sweltering summer weather and his disturbing thoughts of a woman he shouldn't want, but did.

Honey had no way of knowing her presence here had been carefully staged. His brothers had manipulated things so that she had no reason, and no way, to leave. Between Gabe toying with her car and Jordan supplying her everything she could possibly need from town, she'd had no reason to step foot off his property, which was how his brothers had planned it.

He appreciated their efforts, but they couldn't know what it was costing him.

Honey suddenly straightened and put her hands on her shapely hips. She glared at Gabe suspiciously while a sunbeam slanting through a high window in the large shed got caught in her fair hair, forming a halo. "Are you sure you know what you're doing?"

Gabe grinned and touched the tip of her nose with a grease-covered finger, leaving a smudge behind. "Of course I know what I'm doing, sweetie. Relax."

They'd all taken to calling her *sweetie* since they insisted on using an endearment, and her name was just that—her name. Honey had laughed and said that at least this way she could be distinguished from the mule and the cat and the various other assorted animals wandering the land.

Today she had on shorts Jordan had brought her. He'd made the purchases to keep Sawyer from taking her to town, afraid that once she was there, she'd find a way to sneak off. And none of them wanted her to do that.

But to Sawyer's mind, Jordan's fashion sense left a lot to be desired. The shorts were *too* short, displaying the long length of her slim legs and emphasizing the roundness of her pert little butt. But when he'd suggested as much, he'd gotten jeered by his brothers, who seemed to take maniacal delight in commenting on his every thought these days.

He still thought the shorts were too short, but he now suffered in silence. Just as he did when she wore the new skimpy cotton tank tops, or the flirty sundresses, or the lightweight summer nightgowns and robe. Then again, he didn't completely approve of any of the things she now wore. Jordan and Gabe had gotten together and figured out a list of everything she'd need, including some very basic female items he'd never have considered in his lust-induced fog. They'd also shown her where to add neccessities to the list kept posted on the front of the fridge. So now, among the items of aftershave and car oil, face cream and fingernail files had been added.

Every day it seemed she became a bigger part of their lives, and he didn't know what he was going to do when she eventually left. Which she would. Because once she was safe, he wouldn't ask her to stay.

Honey, tired of watching Gabe fumble under the hood of her car, turned to flounce out of the shed. When she caught sight of him, her face lit up with a warmth that filled him to overflowing. "Sawyer! I didn't know you were here."

As usual, her eyes ate him up and sexual tension immediately vibrated between them. But she never touched him in front of anyone, too concerned with trying to keep their intimate involvement private. He didn't have the heart to point out his brothers were far from idiots and had already deduced more than he'd ever admitted even to himself. Besides, the fact she touched everyone *but* him was pretty telling, like the drunk who overenunciated to hide his state of inebriation. Honey was what Gabe called a touchy-feely woman, always hugging and patting people she cared about. And she cared about all of them, that was painfully obvious.

It was one of the main reasons his brothers insisted

on prolonging her stay. Not that he'd let her leave anyway until the issue of her safety was resolved.

And that was the topic he brought up now. As she neared, he braced himself and said, "I think you should call your fiancé."

Just like that, the light died in her eyes and her welcome became wary, twisting at his heart. She stalled, her new sandals kicking up dust on the shed floor as she came to a standstill. She tried a sickly smile that made him ache. "My fiancé?"

"Ex-fiancé. This Alden idiot."

Gabe quickly wiped off his hands and strode over to them. "What the hell are you talking about, Sawyer?"

Sawyer rubbed his neck, trying to ease his growing tension. He didn't like the idea much himself. If he had his way, he'd never let her get within shouting distance of the bastard. But he couldn't take the pressure anymore, waiting for something to happen so they could act and put an end to it. And he couldn't seem to keep his hands off her.

To get things settled, they had to force the issue, and calling her ex was the only way he could think of to do it.

He stared down at her and resisted the urge to hold her close. "Morgan and I discussed it. We both still think Alden is involved somehow. You said yourself that his behavior was strange. The only problem is finding the link. If you call him, we can listen in and maybe we'll catch something you missed."

Her expression turned mulish, so he quickly clarified. "I'm not suggesting we're any better at this than you are. But at the time you left, you were upset. Now you're calm, and we're totally detached." Only he wasn't. He was in so far, he didn't know if he'd ever see daylight again. He cleared his throat and forged on. "Between us we might pick up a small detail that will make sense. I know the waiting is hard on you."

She nodded slowly, her eyes never leaving his face. "I was just telling Gabe that I think I should stop imposing on you all."

His stomach knotted. "And no doubt Gabe told you that was nonsense."

"Well, yes."

Gabe put his arm around her shoulders. "Damn right I did. She's not going anywhere until we know it's safe."

"And this is the best way to find out if it is or not," Sawyer replied, trying to ignore the way Gabe held her and the hot jealousy he couldn't deny. The only male who could touch her without setting off his possessive alarms was his son. And it was a good thing, since Casey seemed even more inclined than the rest to dote on her. Sawyer was almost certain Casey had his own agenda in mind, but unlike the others, Casey wasn't as easy to figure out. He'd always been a mature kid, proud and too smart for his own good, but he'd never been overly demonstrative with anyone but the family. In fact, he was usually more closed off, keeping his thoughts and feelings private. The way he'd so openly accepted Honey was enough to raise a few brows.

"You plan to set some bait?" Gabe asked, pulling Honey even closer as if to shield her. From Sawyer.

He scowled and nudged Gabe away, looping his own arm around Honey and hauling her up possessively against him, regardless of her chagrined struggle. "Not exactly bait. You know I wouldn't endanger her. But I want her to come right out and tell the bastard that she's been followed, that she's in hiding, that she damn well might go to the police despite her father's absurd edict if she doesn't get some answers. There's a good chance Alden will slip up and give something away."

Gabe gave a thoughtful nod. "It's not a bad plan. If he's innocent, we should be able to tell, don't you think?"

"I would hope."

Honey stepped away from both men. "Do I have any say-so in this?"

Sawyer looked at her warily. In the past two weeks he'd come to learn her moods well. Right now she was plenty peeved, and when Honey wasn't happy, she had no qualms about letting them all know it. The fact that she was one small woman in a household of five large men didn't appear to intimidate her one bit. "Uh...sure."

"Then *no.* I'm not doing it. What if Alden is at the heart of it all? What if he traces the call? He's certainly capable of doing that. Then the trouble could land right here at your own front door."

"And you still don't trust us to take care of you?" His temper started a slow boil; this was a constant bone of contention between them. "You think we're all so helpless we'd let someone hurt you? That *I'd* let anyone hurt you?"

In a sudden burst of temper, she went on tiptoes and

jutted her chin at Sawyer. "I'm not thinking of me, dammit! *I'm thinking of you and your family!*"

Gabe glanced at Sawyer, a comical look of disbelief on his face. "She's trying to protect us?"

Sawyer crossed his arms over his chest and nodded, thoroughly bemused and annoyed. "Looks that way."

Throwing her hands into the air, Honey shouted, "You're not invincible!"

Sawyer rolled his eyes to the heavens. He wanted to shake her, and he wanted to take her back into the shed, slam the door on the world and make love to her again. Just that morning, right before dawn, he'd slipped into her bed and attempted to rouse her with gentle kisses and touches. But things always turned wild with Honey, no matter his resolve. When he'd left the room for his office shortly after seven o'clock, he'd been totally spent, and his legs had been shaking from the vigorous lovemaking they'd indulged in. Honey had gone soundly back to sleep. He'd never known a person who could sleep as hard and sound as she did. She'd be awake one moment, gone the next, especially after sex. A marching band could go through the room, and she wouldn't stir so much as an eyelash.

Now, it felt like months since he'd touched her. He turned away. "We're not dealing with organized crime, sweetheart. Buckhorn is a small county without a lot of need for reinforcements. It's natural for us to rely on ourselves to take care of problems whenever possible. But until we figure out exactly who is after you, we're helpless. Getting more information is the only sensible thing to do."

She looked ready to kick dirt at him, then she turned

on her heel and stomped back to the shed. Gabe stared after her. She went to the back of the car and opened the trunk.

"I can't keep messing with her car much longer. She's starting to get suspicious. If I don't fix it soon, she'll figure it out, or else she'll decide I'm an inept idiot. I don't relish either prospect."

Sawyer's smile was grim. "Yeah, you must've changed everything that can be changed by now."

"Just about. Changing a few parts that had to be ordered was a stroke of genius, if I say so myself." Gabe shrugged. "I don't think she knows it's in better running order now than ever, but to be on the safe side, I took a few wires off in case she decides to give it a try. I'm still not willing to trust her to stay put."

"We can't keep her here forever."

Gabe rubbed some grease off his thumb, trying to look indifferent. But Sawyer heard the calculating tone to his words. "I don't see why not."

Sawyer sighed. "Because this isn't her home. She has a sister who's dying to see her again, despite the reassurances Honey gave her over the phone." Honey had called her sister, Misty, the morning she'd accepted the fact they wouldn't let her leave while there was danger. Misty had been relieved that her sister was safe, and very curious about the men she was staying with. Sawyer had spoken a few words with her, trying to allay her concerns. Misty had a husky voice and a lot of loyalty. Sawyer had liked her instantly.

"She can call her sister again. That's not a problem. Or better yet, her sister could visit her here."

All the brothers were curious about Misty Malone,

much to Honey's amusement. Sawyer sighed. "She also has some issues she needs to resolve with her father."

"Ha! I personally think she'd be better off never laying eyes on the man again."

"If everything she's told us is accurate, then I'd agree. But I've never met the man and I have no idea what motivates him."

"You're defending him?"

Sawyer understood Gabe's disbelief. From what she'd said, Honey's father wasn't an easy man to like. "You've met Honey. You've gotten to know her in the last few weeks. Do you honestly believe any male could be so immune to her, but especially her father?"

Gabe seemed to chew that over. "I see what you mean. She's such a sweetheart, she's hard to resist. No, I can't imagine a man, any man, not loving her on sight."

Sawyer felt those words like a sucker punch in the solar plexus. It took his breath away. "I wasn't talking about love, dammit."

With a pitying look, Gabe shook his head. "Be glad you staked a claim first, Sawyer, because just about anyone else would be more than glad to talk about love. Maybe you should remember that while you're being so pigheaded."

It took two steps for Sawyer to be chest to chest with his youngest brother. Through his teeth, he growled, "Just what the hell is that supposed to mean?"

Gabe didn't back down, but then Sawyer would have been surprised if he had. Instead, he took a step closer so they almost touched, and his eyes narrowed. "It means, you stubborn ass, that she's—"

Honey suddenly shoved herself between them. She had a large box in her hands, and her scowl was hotter than the blazing sunshine. "Don't you two start! I've got enough to worry about right now without having to listen to you bicker!"

Flustered, Sawyer glared one more time at Gabe then forcefully took the box from Honey. "Men don't bicker."

"Ha! You were both muttering low and growling and acting like bulldogs facing off over a meaty bone. It's absurd for brothers to carry on that way."

Gabe blinked at her. "We were just...uh, discussing things."

"Uh-huh. Like what?"

Sawyer stared at her, stymied for just a moment, then he hefted the box. "What the hell have you got in here?"

Sidetracked, she said, "My stereo stuff. It's been in the trunk. Thank goodness nothing got wet when I went in the lake. Since I've had no reason to listen to music lately, I'd almost forgotten about it—until Casey and I decided to dance."

Gabe muffled a startled laugh. "You're going to *what?*"

She sniffed in disdain at his attitude. "Dance. To *my* music. What you men listen to is appalling."

Gabe trotted along beside them as Sawyer started toward the house with the box. "It's called country and it's damn good."

She made a face. "Yes, well, I prefer rock and roll."

"This oughta be good."

Her gaze turned to Gabe. "You plan to watch?"

"Hell, yes."

"If you do," she warned, as if she could make him reconsider, "you'll have to dance, too."

"Wouldn't miss it."

Sawyer marched through the back door, through the kitchen, down the hall and into the family room. The stereo was on a built-in shelf beside the huge stone fireplace centered on the outside wall. The speakers hung from the pine walls in four locations beneath the cathedral ceiling. This room wasn't carpeted, but instead had a large area rug in a Native American motif that covered the middle of the polished wood floor. Facing the front of the house, it had a wall of windows reaching to the ceiling, shaded by the enormous elms out front. Two comfortable couches, a variety of padded armchairs and some eclectic tables handmade from area denizens filled the room.

The first time they'd all gotten together and played music and chess and arm wrestled, in general goofing off and relaxing, Honey had looked agog at all the noise. Their boisterous arguments over the chess match, more intense than those over the wrestling, almost drowned out the country songs, and she had winced as if in pain. After half an hour she'd claimed a headache and said she was going down by the lake to sit on the dock and enjoy the evening air and quiet.

Sawyer had promptly followed her, ignoring the gibes of his brothers and Casey's ear-to-ear grin. Knowing he wouldn't be interrupted, not when they all worked so hard at conniving just such a situation for him, he'd made love to her under the stars. Dew from the lake had dampened their heated bodies, and Honey's soft moans were enhanced by the sounds of gentle waves lapping at the shore. Now, looking at her face, he could tell she was remembering, too.

He dropped the box and took a step toward her. Her eyes suddenly looked heavy, the pulse in her throat raced, her skin flushed. Damn, he was getting hard.

Casey hit him in the back. "Snap out of it, Dad. I'm too young to see this, and Uncle Gabe is about to fall down laughing."

Sawyer scowled at Gabe, who lifted his hands innocently even though his shoulders were shaking with mirth, then he turned to Casey and couldn't help but chuckle. "Where did you come from?"

"Well, according to you and that talk we had when I was seven—"

Sawyer put him a headlock and mussed his hair. "Smart ass. You know that wasn't what I meant."

The second Casey twisted free, laughing, Honey stepped forward and smoothed his hair back down. And he let her, grinning the whole time. Casey was a good head and a half taller than Honey, with shoulders almost twice as wide. Yet he let her mother on him. And every damn time she did, something inside Sawyer softened to the point of pain. He loved Casey so much, had loved him from the first second he'd held him as a squalling, red-faced infant, regardless of all the issues present, that anyone else who loved him automatically earned a place in his heart.

She finished with Casey's hair and gave him a hug of

greeting. Sawyer felt ridiculously charmed once again—and he hated it.

"I brought in my music," she told Casey, as if any reprieve from country music was the equivalent of being spared the gallows. Casey hadn't yet told her he actually liked country. "You want to take a look, see if anything interests you?"

"That'd be great. I'll check them out as soon as I've washed up."

Gabe stood to stretch. "You get everything taken care of, Case?"

He nodded, then turned to Sawyer. "When Mrs. Hartley left here today, I saw she was limping."

Sawyer pulled his thoughts away from Honey with an effort. "She twisted her ankle the other day rushing in from her car when it was raining."

"She told me. So I followed her over there to help her out. I got her grass cut and did some weeding, then went to the grocery for her." To Honey, he said, "Mrs. Hartley is close to seventy, and she's real sweet. She's the librarian in town, and she orders in the books I like."

Honey laced her fingers together at her waist and beamed at Casey. "What a thoughtful thing to do! I'm so proud of you."

Casey actually blushed. "Uh, it was no big deal. Anyone would have done the same."

"That's not true." Honey's smile was gentle, warm. "The world is filled with selfish people who never think of others."

The men exchanged glances. They really didn't think too much of helping out, since it was second nature to them. But Sawyer supposed to Honey it did seem generous, given the men she'd known.

Gabe saved Casey from further embarrassment by throwing an arm around him and hustling him along. "Go get washed so we can put the music on. I'm getting anxious." He winked at Honey, and then they were gone.

The family room had open archways rather than doors that could be closed, so they weren't afforded any real privacy, but already Sawyer felt the strain of being alone with her. He looked at her with hot eyes and saw she was studying some of the framed photos on the wall. There were pictures of all of them, but the majority were of Casey at every age.

Sawyer came up behind her and kissed her nape. He felt desperate to hold her, to stave off time, and he looped his arms around her. "Mmm. You smell good."

He could feel her smile, hear it in her response. "You always say that."

"Because you always smell so damn good." He nipped her ear. "It makes me crazy."

She leaned against him, and her tone turned solemn. "You've done an excellent job with Casey. I don't think I've ever known a more giving, understanding or mature kid. He's serious, but still fun-loving, sort of a mix of all of you. He's incredible." She leaned her head back to smile up at Sawyer. "But then, he inherited some pretty incredible genes, being your son."

Sawyer's arms tightened for the briefest moment, making her gasp, then he released her. He shoved his hands into his back pockets and paced away. Maybe, considering he had insisted she call her fiancé tonight, he should at least explain a few things.

Honey touched his arm. "What is it?"

"Casey's not really mine." He no sooner said it than he shook his head. "That is, he's mine in every way that counts. But I didn't father him. I don't know who his father is—and neither did his mother."

"WHAT DID YOU SAY?"

Sawyer laughed at himself. He made no sense, so her confusion was expected. "My wife cheated. A lot. She didn't like my long hours studying, or my distraction with school in general. By the time Casey was born, I'd already filed for a divorce. It wasn't easy for her. She had no family, and she wasn't happy about the divorce. In fact, she was crushed by it. She pleaded with me not to leave her, but she...well, once I knew she'd been with other men, I couldn't forgive her. I understood it, but I couldn't forgive."

Honey wrapped her arms around him from behind, leaning her head on his back. She didn't say anything, just held onto him.

"I'd been sort of taking care of her for a long time, since high school even. Her parents died when she was seventeen, and an aunt took her in, but then she died, too, when Ashley was nineteen. She never had a job, and the idea of getting one horrified her. I just...I dunno. It seemed logical to marry her, to take care of her. We'd been dating forever, and I felt sorry for her, and there was no one else I wanted."

Honey kissed his back, showing her understanding. "Why did she cheat?"

Sawyer shrugged. "Hell, I don't know. She seemed

plenty satisfied with..." He stalled, casting her a quick look.

"She seemed satisfied with you sexually? Of course she did. You're an incredible man, Sawyer." Her small hands were flat on his abdomen, making him catch his breath as she idly stroked him, meaning to offer comfort, but arousing him instead. All she had to do was breathe to turn him on; her touch made him nearly incoherent with lust.

"You're also an incredible lover," she added huskily, making his muscles twitch. "No woman would have complaints."

He looked away again. When she said things like that, it made him want to toss her on the couch and strip her clothes off. He reacted like an uncivilized barbarian, ready to conquer. Feeling a tad uncomfortable with that analogy, he rushed through the rest of his explanation. "She told me she felt neglected, so she cheated. And then she couldn't understand why I wouldn't forgive her, because in her mind, it was my fault. I filed for divorce, but then I found out she was several months pregnant. She was angry and taunted me with the fact it wasn't mine. But by then, I hardly cared. It was an embarrassment, but little else."

"Did everyone know?"

"Not at first. She got over being mad and just started pleading with me to take her back. She fought the damn divorce tooth and nail. I tried to be considerate with her, but I was also in the middle of med school and I had my hands full. When she went into labor, she begged me to go the hospital with her." He got quiet as he remembered that awful day, his guilt, his feelings of helplessness. His family had wanted to be supportive, but no one knew what to do. The entire town had watched the drama unfold, and it was painful.

"There was no one else," he murmured, "and I couldn't leave her there alone. So I went. And after they handed me Casey, Ashley told me she was putting him up for adoption."

He shook his head, once again feeling the utter disbelief. After holding Casey for just a few short hours, he knew he wouldn't let him go. It wasn't the baby's fault his mother had been discontent in her marriage, and while wonderful adoptions existed, he wouldn't put it to the chance.

He pulled away from Honey and went to stare blindly at a photo of Casey as a toddler. In a hoarse tone, he admitted, "I signed the birth certificate, claiming him as my own, and dared her to fight me on it." His throat felt tight, and he swallowed hard. "We're not without influence here. My family has been a force since my father's days, and Ashley knew in a battle she didn't stand a chance. She hadn't wanted Casey, and I damn sure did, so she reluctantly agreed. For awhile, she was bitter about it. I don't know who all she complained to, but everyone around here knew the whole private story within days. They knew, but they didn't dare say anything."

Honey didn't approach him this time. She kept her distance and spoke in a whisper. "Where's his mother now?"

"I'm not sure. She got ostracized by the town, not because of me, because I swear I tried to make it easy on her. But she was bitter and that bitterness set everyone against her. She moved away, and last I heard, she'd remarried and moved to England. That was years ago.

Casey knows the truth, and I've tried to help him understand her and her decisions. And my own."

"You feel responsible."

He turned to face her. "I can't excuse myself from it, Honey. I played a big part in her actions. She resented my sense of obligation to others, and I resented her interference in my life. I *like* taking care of people, and I like being a doctor, yet that's what drove her away. She wanted more of my time, and I didn't want to give it to her, not if it meant taking away from my family and the community."

"And you don't ever want a wife to...interfere that way again?"

"I don't want to run the risk of another scandal. I haven't changed."

Her smile was gentle as she crossed the floor and hugged herself up against him. "There's no reason you should. You accept the influence of your name, but also the responsibility of it, like a liege lord, and you handle that responsibility well. If Ashley didn't understand, it's not your fault."

"She was my wife."

"She was also a grown woman who made her own terrible decisions. I can only imagine how you felt, with everyone knowing the truth, but I'm sure no one blames you."

"I blame myself."

She burrowed against him, her small body pressed tight to his own. Damn, but he wanted her.

All his life he'd been surrounded by family and neighbors and friends. That wouldn't change, but he knew when Honey left, he'd feel alone. And for the first time in his life he felt vulnerable, a feeling he instinctively fought against.

He wrapped his fist in her hair and turned her face up for his kiss. She tried to dodge his mouth, wanting to talk, to instruct him on his sense of obligation, but he wouldn't allow it. With a low growl, he held her closer and roughly took her mouth, pushing his tongue inside, stemming any protest she might make.

Just as she always did, Honey kissed him back with equal enthusiasm. Her hands clutched his shirt, and she went on her tiptoes to seal the space between them.

Sawyer groaned. He pulled his mouth free and kissed her throat, her chin. "I hate feeling like this," he said, meaning the way his need for her consumed him beyond reason. There were so many other things to consider right now, and all he wanted to do was get inside her.

Honey pressed her fingers to his mouth, and though she smiled, her eyes looked damp. "You feel responsible for me, and you're trying to do the right thing, because that's who you are. You help people by giving. You take in strays, both people and animals."

"The animals are Jordan's."

"But they're accepted by you. By all of you. Your wife was a stray. I'm a stray."

He grasped her arms and shook her slightly. "Dammit, Honey, I care about you."

She gave a soft, sad chuckle. "You care about everyone, Sawyer. But I don't want or need anyone to take care of me. This time, you aren't responsible."

"I wasn't making comparisons, dammit." His frustration level shot through the roof as he tried to find a balance for the feelings.

"I know." Her hand cupped his jaw, her eyes filled with emotion. "I won't lie and tell you I don't want a family. I was willing to marry a despicable creep like Alden for it, and he couldn't offer half what you do with your nosy, domineering brothers and your incredible son and your unshakable honor. But I have no intentions of clinging to a loveless relationship. I tried that with Alden, and look where it got me." She smiled, then shook her head. "I've been thinking about it, and I decided I deserve to be loved. I deserve a family of my own, and a happily ever after. I would never settle for anything less now."

Her words left him empty, made him want to protect her, to ask her to stay forever. But the one time he'd tried marriage it had been for all the wrong reasons. Now, he wanted Honey horribly, but he just didn't know about love, not a romantic, everlasting love. All he knew for certain was the uncontrollable lust that drove him wild.

She looked up into his face, her eyes soft, her expression softer, then she sighed. "Don't look so stern, Sawyer. You haven't done anything wrong. You didn't make me any false promises, and you didn't take advantage of me." Her teeth sank into her bottom lip to stop it from trembling. "All you did was show me how men can and should be. And for that, more than anything, I thank you."

She stepped away and drew a deep breath. "So, now that we've cleared that up, what do you say I make that phone call?"

He wanted to say to hell with it; he wanted to shake her for being so nonchalant about her own feelings.

Trying for a detachment he didn't possess, he

glanced at his watch. "Morgan should be home soon. Then we'll call."

From the open doorway, Morgan growled, "I'm home now."

Sawyer looked up and saw his brother lounging there, arms crossed belligerently over his chest, his eyes narrowed and his jaw set. He looked like a thundercloud. How much had he heard? Obviously enough, given his extra-ferocious scowl.

First Gabe, and now Morgan. They didn't approve of his methods, his urgency in getting the issue resolved. Despite what he'd told Gabe and Honey, Morgan had argued with him over the idea of contacting Alden. Morgan had called him an ass for denying that he cared. Sawyer had countered that he'd only known her for a little over two weeks, which had made Morgan snort in derision. *You knew Ashley for a short lifetime, but that didn't make the relationship any better.* Truthful words that had been gnawing at him all day.

Sawyer abruptly headed for the doorway to call Gabe and Jordan in, determined to blot Morgan's warning from his mind. Once the brothers were all collected, Sawyer noticed Honey wouldn't quite meet his gaze. It was as if she'd shut him out, already removing herself from him. He hated it, but told himself it was for the best.

The brothers were setting up the extra phones in the room so they'd all be able to listen in the hopes of catching a clue. Casey had Honey's collection of music pulled toward him, idly thumbing through CDs and tapes. Sawyer doubted there'd be any dancing tonight, but he understood Casey's need for a distraction.

Then Casey nudged Honey. "What's this?"

Absently, she glanced down, frowning at a plain tape with the word *Insurance* written on it. "I don't know."

Sawyer, hoping to ease her tension, said, "We'll be a few minutes yet if you want to check it out."

Casey carried the tape to the stereo and put it in. With the very first words spoken on the tape, a crushing stillness settled over the room. Murmured conversations and quiet preparations ceased, as slowly, everyone stopped what they were doing to listen.

Her gaze glued to the stereo as if transfixed, Honey whispered, "Sawyer," and he was by her side in an instant, taking her hand, as appalled as she.

The voices were unrecognizable to Sawyer, other than being male. But what they were discussing was painfully obvious: murder. And the fact that Honey knew the voices was easy to see by her horrified expression.

So you'll do it?

It won't be a problem. But we'll need some good-faith money upfront.

I can give you half now, the rest after she marries me and her father is gone. But remember, you have to wait for my instructions. If you kill the old man before the legalities are taken care of, I won't get a damn thing. Which means you won't get a thing.

How long are we talking?

A week or two. It's already in his will, but I want to make sure there won't be any mix-ups.

Honey turned wounded eyes to Sawyer. "That's Alden."

Sawyer pulled her closer, but her face remained blank, white with hurt and disbelief. One by one, his brothers and Casey gathered around her until she was listening to the tape from behind a wall of protective men.

You just make sure the wedding goes off without a hitch. I don't want to be wasting my time here.

I can handle the bride. Don't worry about that.

What if she objects to her daddy being snuffed? Will the conditions of the will alter if she divorces you?

No, she's completely clueless to my plans, so don't worry about her. She won't have any idea that I was behind it all. If anything, she'll want me to comfort her.

There was some masculine chuckling over that, and one of the men mumbled, *An added bonus, huh?*

Sawyer shot to his feet, his fists clenched, the corners of his vision clouded by rage. "I'll kill him."

Morgan grabbed Sawyer's shoulder. "Don't be stupid."

"Or so human," Gabe added, staring at him in fascination. "It shocks me. You're usually such a damn saint."

Honey slowly stood and faced them all. "I...I have to call the police."

Sawyer squeezed his eyes shut and tried to find his control. Gabe was right—he was acting out of character. He was the pacifist in the family, yet all he wanted to do was get Alden close enough to beat him to a pulp.

Morgan stepped around Sawyer. "Honey, I think you should still make that call."

She blinked owlishly, as if coming out of a daze. Feeling grim, Sawyer nodded. "We need to find out who the hell he hired."

Casey stood beside Honey, one arm around her waist. "He made the tape for insurance, just as it says, didn't he? He couldn't take the chance that the men he'd hired would go against him. Or maybe he planned to blackmail them later with it."

Morgan shrugged. "Who the hell knows. The man's obviously an idiot as well as a bastard."

"But why were they after me?"

She looked so lost, everyone was quiet for a moment, trying to find a gentle way to explain it to her.

Sawyer cleared his throat, taking on the duty. "Honey, when you left Alden, you fouled up all the plans. Not only did you make it impossible for him to recoup the money through the marriage, but when you packed up, you evidently took his tape by mistake."

"It...it was with my things. I just sort of shoved everything into a box. I was angry and not really paying attention."

"Exactly. I don't know why he would have hidden the tape among your things, but—"

"Oh, God, he didn't." She clutched at Sawyer, eyes wide. "When I pulled the stereo out, there was a tape shoved up against the wall behind it. Alden only has CDs so I assumed it wasn't his, and I just threw it in with the others."

"But now you have it, and it's evidence not only against the men after you, but against Alden, too. I imagine he had to tell them about it, knowing you'd find it sooner or later and they'd all go to jail. They have to get you, to get the tape."

Honey covered her mouth with a hand, then turned for the phone. "I need to call my father to make sure he's okay. And my sister—"

She looked so panicked, Sawyer gently folded her close, despite her struggles, and held her. "Baby, listen to me. You spoke with Misty yesterday, remember? If anything had been wrong, she'd have told you."

He felt her relax slightly, the rigidity seeping out of her spine. "Yes, of course you're right."

She drew a deep breath, and slowly, right before his eyes, Sawyer watched her pull herself together. She'd been given a terrible blow, but already her shoulders were squared, her expression settling into lines of determination. She stepped away from him. "Let's get this over with. I want to talk to Alden, to find out what I can, and then we can have the police pick him up. The tape will be enough evidence, don't you think?"

Morgan gave one hard nod. "Damn right, especially with the break-in at your sister's and the way you've been chased. But with any luck, he'll incriminate himself further on the phone, and we'll all be witnesses. Don't worry, Honey. It's almost over with. I have friends with the state police who can handle everything."

Sawyer didn't want to let her go, didn't want her to so much as speak to Alden, much less carry on a deceptive conversation, but she was adamant. When she turned her back and walked away from him, it was all he could do not to haul her back up to his side and tote her out of the room.

Honey took a seat by the phone, looking like a queen surrounded by her subjects, and she dialed Alden's number. It took several rings for him to answer, and when he finally did, Honey closed her eyes. "Hello, Alden."

There was a heavy pause. "Honey? Is that you?"

"Yes."

Another pause, then, *"Where the hell have you been?"*

Honey started, but in the next instant she scowled and tightened her hand on the phone. Sawyer felt a swell of pride for her courage.

"Have you been looking for me?"

"You're goddamned right, I've been looking for you. For God's sake, Honey, *I thought you were dead.*"

HONEY STARED at the phone, her entire body trembling with rage. "Why would you think that, Alden? I left because I didn't want to marry you. Didn't you read my note?"

Her calm tone seemed to sink in to him. She heard him breathing heavily in an effort to control himself. "Yes, I read it. Where are you, Honey?"

She stared at her hands on the desk, not at the men who watched her so closely. "I'm afraid, Alden. Someone has been chasing after me."

He muttered low, then said in sugary tones, "Have you spoken with anyone?"

"About what? Our breakup?"

"About... Dammit, never mind that. Where are you living now? I'll come get you."

"I'm not living anywhere." In a calculated lie, she said, "I've been so afraid, just running from whoever is after me. I haven't had a chance to unpack. My clothes were all left at my sister's, but everything else is still in boxes in my trunk. I shouldn't have left, Alden. My father doesn't believe someone is after me, so I can't go to him."

"I know," he answered in soothing tones. "He's never been overly concerned for you. But I am, sweetheart. You know that. I wanted to marry you long before I learned about his will. If you want, we'll make him change it. He can leave everything to your sister. I don't care about the money, I just want you back with me, safe and sound. Tell me where you are so I can come get you."

"I don't know...." She tried to put just the right amount of hesitation into her tone.

"Listen to me, damn you!" He made a sound of pain and cursed. "People *are* after you, and they're dangerous. I know because they already put me in the hospital once. I spent almost a week there and I can tell you it wasn't pleasant!"

Honey glanced at Sawyer and saw his dark eyes glint with satisfaction. She held no sympathy for Alden, either, but knowing they'd hurt him scared her spitless. She didn't want the men anywhere near Sawyer or his family. "Why would anyone hurt you, Alden?"

"I don't know. I think it might have something to do with a shady deal your father made to buy some inside corporate information."

Honey raised her brows. That was an excellent lie, because it was one she would have believed. She made sounds of understanding, and Alden continued. "They won't hesitate to do the same to you, Honey. Let me bring you home where I can protect you while we sort this all out."

Sawyer covered the mouthpiece. "Tell him to meet you here tomorrow." He handed her a piece of paper that Morgan had slipped to him. Honey stared down at the address, recognizing that the location was an area on the outskirts of Buckhorn. Numbly, she shook her head, knowing he planned to put himself in danger. "No."

"No what?" Alden tried cajoling. "Listen to me, Honey. I know you feel betrayed. And I'm sorry. I really do care for you—"

"Let me think, Alden!"

Sawyer walked over to her and gripped her shoulder. He shoved the paper toward her again, then whispered low, "Trust us, Honey. Tell him."

They were all looking at her, waiting. How in the world could she do this to them? She loved each of them. Then Morgan gave her the most furious face she'd ever seen on a human. He reached into his pocket and pulled out his sheriff's badge, flashing it at her as if to remind her this was his job, as if her hesitation had insulted him mightily.

Jordan shrugged at her, and he, too, spoke in a faint whisper. "Either you have him come here, on our own home ground where Morgan has some legal leverage, or we go after him. It's your decision."

She narrowed her eyes at the lot of them. Bullies every one. They had the nasty habit of ganging up on her whenever it suited them.

Alden suddenly asked, "Who's with you?" and suspicion laced his tone.

Knowing she had no choice and hating Alden for it, she did as the brothers asked. "I'm in a diner in a small town in southern Kentucky." She glanced at the note again, then said, "You can meet me in Buckhorn at the town landfill at nine o'clock tomorrow morning. It's...it's deserted. There won't be anyone around."

Sawyer nodded and whispered, "Good girl," and she elbowed him hard. He rubbed his stomach and scowled at her.

"Can you give me directions, sweetheart?" Alden

sounded anxious, and Honey's stomach knotted with dread even as she did as he asked.

"Just hang on until tomorrow morning, darling. You'll feel safer as soon as I get you home."

Though she nearly choked on it, she said, "Thank you," and after she hung up the phone, she glared at all the men, but concentrated most of her ire on Sawyer. "I hope you're happy," she meant to growl, but what emerged was a pathetic wail quickly followed by tears. The brothers looked appalled, and Sawyer, his face softening with sympathy, reached for her. Honey knew if he so much as touched her she'd completely fall apart, so she ran from the room.

She didn't want him to confront Alden. She didn't want him in danger. At the moment, she wished she'd never laid eyes on him. At least then she'd know he would stay safe, and because she loved him so damn much, even though he didn't feel the same, his safety was the only thing that seemed to matter.

She wanted to pretend sleep when Sawyer crept into the dark bedroom hours later, but she was shaking so bad, he knew right away she was awake. He sat on the side of the bed and smoothed his hand over her cheek.

"Are you all right, sweetheart?"

"Yes. Did you make all your plans?"

His hesitation was like an alarm, making her sit up. "Tell me, Sawyer."

"You'll stay here with Casey and Gabe."

"No. If you insist on doing this..."

"I do. Morgan has alerted the state police, and once Alden shows up, we'll grab him. There's no reason to worry."

"Like you wouldn't if you were left behind!"

"Honey..."

She hated acting like a desperate ninny, but she was choking on her helplessness, and she didn't like it. "If Morgan and the police have it in hand, why do you need to go?"

"Because he hurt you."

His quiet words nearly crumbled her heart. She launched herself at him and knocked him backward on the bed. "Sawyer."

He couldn't answer because she was kissing him, his face, his throat, his ear. Sawyer chuckled softly and tried to hold her still, but she reared back and tugged on the fastening to his pants. Surprised, but more than willing, Sawyer lifted his hips and helped her to get his pants off, removing his underwear at the same time. Honey stretched out over him, relishing the feel of his hot, hard flesh. She loved him so much, she wanted to absorb him, his caring, his strength and honor.

Sawyer groaned as she pressed against his pelvis, rocking gently. She felt the immediate rise of his erection along with his accelerated breaths. "Honey, slow down."

She had no intention of listening to him. Moving quickly to the side, she caressed him from shoulders to hip. His hands fell to the mattress, and his body stiffened. Honey bent and kissed his chest. "I love how you feel, Sawyer, how you smell, and how you...taste."

He caught his breath, then let it out in a whoosh when her mouth began trailing kisses down his chest to his abdomen. Both of his hands cupped her head, his fingers tangling gently in her long hair.

Her hand wrapped tightly around his erection, hold-

ing him secure, giving him fair warning of her intent.
She heard a low growl and knew it was Sawyer.

Rubbing her face over his muscled abdomen, she
whispered, "You know how you've done this to me?"

"This?" The word was a strangled gasp.

"Mmm, *this*," she clarified, and lightly ran her
tongue down the length of his penis.

"Damn." His entire body jerked and strained, his
hands tightening in her hair.

"And...this." She gently raked her teeth over him,
down and then back up again.

"*Honey.*"

"And this." His body lurched as her mouth closed
hotly around him. She'd had no idea that pleasuring
him would pleasure her, as well, but her heart raced
with the incredible scent and taste of him and the muttered roughness of his curses. He slowly guided her
head, his entire body drawn taut, his heels digging
hard into the mattress.

She had no real idea how to proceed—she'd never
done this before—but it seemed he enjoyed everything,
so she supposed her inexperience didn't matter. But
before long he was pulling her away despite her pro-
tests.

"You're a witch," he growled, then tucked her beneath him after hastily donning a condom. He entered
her with one solid thrust, and she bit back a loud moan
of acute sensation. As he moved over, his rhythm
smooth and deep, he watched her face. "You liked doing that, didn't you?"

The room was dark, but moonlight spilled over the
bed through the French doors, and she could see the in-

tent expression on his face, how his eyes seemed to glow.

She licked her lips and felt his thrusts deepen. "Very much." Smoothing a hand over his back, she asked, "Do you like doing it to me?"

He froze for a heartbeat, struggling for control, then with a vicious curse he wrapped her up tight, holding her as close as he could get her. "Hell, yes, I like it," he growled. His thrusts were suddenly hard and fast and frantic, and when she cried out, her entire body flooding with sensation, he joined her.

And through it all, his arms were around her, and she heard him whisper again. "I like it too much."

JORDAN STUCK his head in the door but kept his gaze judiciously on the ceiling. He spoke in a near silent murmur. "I hate to interrupt all this extracurricular activity, but you didn't hear my knock and we have visitors."

Sawyer immediately lifted away from Honey, and answered in the same quiet hush. "Who?"

"I don't know for sure. I was in my room about to bed down when I heard a noise. I looked out and saw someone in the shed. If I don't miss my guess, good old Alden called in the muscle. His bully boys are probably looking for the tape in her car."

"Goddammit," Sawyer hissed, angry at himself, "we should have thought of that." Sawyer was out of the bed in an instant and pulling on his pants.

Honey threw herself against his back, wrapping her arms tight around him. "No, Sawyer, just stay inside!"

"Shh." He took a moment to gently pry her hands loose and kiss her forehead. "It's all right, sweetheart."

Since she was barely covered by the sheet and evidently didn't care, it was a good thing Jordan had averted his face. He said without looking at her, "Morgan has called in the troops, sweetie, so don't get all frantic on me."

Sawyer had assumed as much, but he saw it didn't ease Honey at all. He glanced sharply at Jordan. "Casey?"

"I sent him to the basement. Gabe is with him, and they're waiting on her."

He nodded. "Come on, Honey. You need to get your robe."

"Don't do this, Sawyer."

Her pleading tone unnerved him, but he hardened himself against it. He'd do what he had to to protect her. "There's no time for this, babe. Come on, have a little trust, okay?"

She moved reluctantly, but she did scoot off the bed and put her arms into the robe he held for her. Wearing only his slacks, Sawyer followed Jordan out, keeping Honey safely at his back. "How did they know she was here?"

"Maybe Alden had the phone call traced, or maybe someone in town knows and spilled the beans. She's been here a couple of weeks now, and you've had a line of patients every day. And Honey, once you've seen her, isn't exactly a woman to forget."

Sawyer grunted at that. She was so damn sexy she made his muscles go into spasms. Jordan was right; no one would forget her, and her description would be easy enough to peg.

When they neared the basement steps, Gabe was

there waiting. "You owe me for this one, Sawyer. You know how I hate missing all the action."

"Keep her safe, and you can name your price."

Gabe grinned at that. "If you get a chance, punch the bastards once for me."

He handed Honey over to his brother. She hadn't said another word, and she wouldn't look at him. Gabe gently put his arm around her. "Come on, sweetie. Casey is looking forward to the company."

"Gabe?" Sawyer waited until his brother met his gaze. "Don't come out, no matter what, until I come for you."

"We'll be fine, Sawyer. Go, but be careful."

Sawyer watched Honey disappear down the steps. She was far too passive to suit him at the moment, but he brushed it off. Morgan was already outside and no doubt could use their help. He closed the basement door, heard Gabe turn the lock, and he and Jordan rushed silently out the back door and across the damp grass. They kept low and in the shadows and they found Morgan just where Sawyer knew he would be, peering around the barn, the closest outbuilding to the shed, keeping the intruders in sight.

"You two sleuths sounded like a herd of elephants."

Morgan's sibilant mutter was filled with disgust, but Sawyer didn't take exception. "Did you see anything?"

"Two men, both big bastards. From the sounds of it, they're getting into Honey's car."

"Looking for the tape."

"I assume. And when they don't find it, they'll head for the house."

"You see any weapons?"

Morgan grunted, but the sound was drowned out by

the myriad night noises, crickets, frogs, rustling tree branches. An eerie fog, visible through the darkness, drifted over the ground. Morgan wiped his forehead, his gaze still trained on the shed. "They'd be total idiots if they weren't armed."

"Jordan said you put the call in to the state police?"

"Yeah." Suddenly he pressed himself back, then glanced at Sawyer. "I don't think they're going to make it on time, though."

Sawyer curled his hands into fists, easily comprehending Morgan's meaning. He was on his haunches, and he tightened his muscles, ready to move. There was no way in hell he was letting anyone near the house, not with Honey and Casey inside.

Morgan reached past him and thrust his gun at Jordan, a silent order for Jordan to be backup. Jordan accepted the gun with a quietly muttered complaint, then braced himself.

Shadows were visible first, then the dark, indistinct forms of two men creeping quietly across the empty yard. They mumbled to each other, then the one trailing slightly behind growled, "That little bitch has been more trouble than she's worth. When I get hold of her—"

Without a word, Morgan launched himself at the first man, who caught the movement too late to turn. Sawyer was right behind him. It gave him enormous satisfaction to hear the grunt of pain from the man who'd threatened Honey as he drove him hard to the ground. His fist connected solidly with a jaw, earning a rank curse before the man shoved him aside with his legs and struggled to his feet. Sawyer faced him, taunting, anxious, confident in his abilities.

And then he heard Gabe shout, and Honey was racing across the yard, distracting Sawyer for just a moment. The man swung, but she got in the way, and his fist clipped her, knocking her to the ground.

Sawyer erupted with blind fury. He stood there heaving just long enough to insure Gabe had Honey in hand and that she was all right. He was barely aware of Morgan pounding a man into the dirt, or of Jordan standing silently in the shadows, the gun drawn. He didn't notice that his son had turned on the floodlights or that the man, knowing he was outnumbered, stood frozen before him, waiting. He'd been dealing with a clamoring swell of emotions all day, pushing him slowly over the edge. And now, seeing Honey hurt, he went into a tailspin. Sawyer felt himself exploding, and with a look of shock, the man raised his fists.

The bastard was large, but not large enough. He was strong, but not strong enough. And he fought dirty, but Sawyer had the advantage of icy rage, and after a few short minutes, Morgan wrapped his arms around Sawyer from behind and pulled him away. "Enough, Sawyer," he hissed into his ear. "The state guys are here and we don't need to put on a show."

He was still shaking with rage, his knuckles bloody, his heart pounding. Slowly, Honey approached him, and Morgan, using caution, released him.

She had a swelling bruise beneath her left eye, but it was the uncertainty in her gaze that nearly felled him. Sawyer opened his arms, and with a small sound she threw herself against him.

He hadn't wanted responsibility for another wife, but ironically, the more Honey insisted on taking care of herself, the more she agreed with his edicts, the more he wanted her. The fact she *didn't* need him, that she was strong and capable and proud, only made her more appealing and made him more determined to coddle her.

Noise surrounded them, questions, chatter. Sawyer heard Morgan giving directions for Alden to be picked up, but none of it mattered to him. He squeezed her tighter and tried not to make a fool of himself by being overly emotional. She'd been hurt so much already. He tipped her back and kissed the bruise on her cheek. "Are you okay?"

Her long hair fell forward to hide her face. "Yes. I'm sorry I got in your way. Gabe told me you'd be likely to skin me for it, after he finished fussing over me."

"What were you doing out here, sweetheart? I told you to stay safe in the basement."

"I snuck out when Gabe wasn't looking." She peered up at him, her expression earnest. "I couldn't stay down there, hiding, while you put yourself in danger for me. I couldn't." Her uncertainty melted away, replaced by a pugnacious frown. "And you shouldn't have asked me to!"

Sawyer fought a smile. "I'm sorry."

She pulled away and paced. The small cat darted out of the bushes to follow her, keeping up with Honey's agitated stride. It was only then Sawyer realized she was wearing Jordan's shirt. Her housecoat, or what he could see of it beneath the shirt, looked nearly transparent under the bright floodlights. He glanced at Jordan, who lounged against the barn wall, his arms crossed over his bare chest. Casey stood beside him, looking agog at the men being handcuffed by a bevy of uniformed officers. Morgan was in the hub of it all, a tall figure of authority.

Gabe reentered the yard with an ice pack and came directly to Honey. "Here, sweetie, put this on your cheek."

Honey ignored him, still pacing, her bare feet now wet and her movements agitated. Sawyer took the pack from Gabe and corralled Honey and started the parade back into the house. They'd all be answering questions soon enough, but for right now, Morgan could handle things.

HOURS LATER, Honey once again found herself seated in the kitchen, the center of attention in the middle of the night. All the men were fussing around her, fretful over a silly bruise that she felt stupid for having. If she hadn't panicked, if she hadn't run into the way of a fist, she wouldn't have been hurt. And after seeing Morgan's and Sawyer's knuckles, her one small injury seemed paltry beyond compare.

She sighed. The men each jumped to her aid, taking that small sound as one of pain.

"Will you all stop hovering?" she groused. "You're making me nervous."

Gabe grinned, finally seeing the hilarity in the situation. "I kinda like doting on you, sweetie. You may as well get used to it."

Honey didn't dare look at Sawyer. She tried for a sunny smile that made her face feel ready to crack. "I don't think that'll be necessary. Thanks to you macho guys, my worries are over. There's no reason for me to keep imposing, or to hang around and get used to your domineering personalities. The police told me I could leave, that when they need me, I'll hear from them. And my sister was so anxious when I called her, I think I should be getting home."

It was as if they'd all turned to statues. Honey managed to eke out one more smile, though it cost her. "Since I don't have much to pack, I can be out of here in the morning. But in case I don't catch any of you before you leave for work, I wanted you to know..." Her throat seemed to close up, and she struggled to hold back her tears. Casey stared at her, his jaw ticking, and she wanted to grab him up and claim him as her own. She swallowed and tried again. But this time her voice was so soft, it could barely be heard. "I wanted you all to know how special you are, and how much I appreciate everything you've done for me."

Jordan and Morgan glared at Sawyer. Gabe got up to pace. Casey, still unflinching, said, "Don't go."

Honey stared down at her folded hands. "I have to, Case. It's safe now, and my family needs me."

Morgan made a rude sound. "Your sister, maybe. But your father? I can't believe you're so quick to forgive him."

"I haven't. But he is my father, and I almost lost him by marrying the wrong man. He was as shocked by it all as I was. He said his lawyers will take care of everything, but we still have a lot to talk about."

"You could stay just a little longer," Jordan suggested, and he, too, looked angry.

"I can't keep hiding here, Jordan. It isn't right."

Morgan walked past Sawyer and deliberately shouldered him, nearly knocking him over. Sawyer cursed and turned to face his brother, but Gabe laughed, diffusing the moment. "Down, Sawyer. The fight is over."

Sawyer stared at him, red-eyed and mean.

Honey didn't quite know what to think of him. He'd fought so...effectively. Yet the brothers claimed he was a pacifist. After the way he'd enjoyed punching that man, Honey had her doubts.

Gabe was still chuckling. "You know, Sawyer, it isn't Morgan's ass you're wanting to kick, but your own."

Sawyer glared a moment more, then pulled out a chair and dropped into it. The brothers seemed to find his behavior hilarious, but Honey couldn't share in their humor. She hurt from the inside out, and trying to keep that pain hidden was wearing on her.

Morgan crossed his arms over his chest. "What if she's pregnant?"

Sawyer's narrowed gaze shot to Honey. She sputtered in surprise. "I'm not pregnant!"

"How do you know?"

"Dammit, Morgan, don't you think a woman knows these things?"

"Sure, after a while, but not this early on."

There was no way she would explain with four pairs of masculine eyes watching her, just how careful Sawyer had been. Through her teeth, she growled, "Take my word on it."

Sawyer stood suddenly, nearly upsetting his chair, and he leaned toward Honey, his battered hands spread flat on the tabletop. He looked furious and anxious and determined. "Would you be opposed to getting pregnant?"

Her mouth opened twice before any words would come out. "*Now?*"

He made an impatient sound. "Eventually."

Not at all sure what Sawyer was getting at, her answer was tentative, but also honest. "No, I wouldn't mind. I want to have children." She stared at him hard. "But only if a man loves me. And only if it's forever."

Sawyer straightened, still keeping his gaze glued to hers. "Would you be opposed to sons, because that seems to be the dominate gene among us."

Honey, too, stood. She bit her lips, feeling her heart start to swell. A laugh bubbled up inside her, and she barely repressed it. "I'm getting used to men and their vagaries."

"Your father would have to change his goddamned will, because I won't take a penny from him, now or ever."

"Absolutely. I already told him that."

"Do you love me?"

There was a collective holding of breath, and she smiled. For such big, strong, confident men, they were certainly uneasy about her answer. "Yes. But...but I don't want your pushy brothers to force you into anything."

That response brought about a round of hilarity, with the brothers shouting, "Ha," and, "Yeah, right," and, "As if we ever could!"

Sawyer rounded the table with a purposeful stride and the brothers got out of his way, still laughing. Casey whooped. Sawyer stopped in front of Honey and whispered, "Damn, I love you," which made her laugh and cry, then he scooped her up in his arms and turned so she faced everyone, and announced formally, "If you'll all excuse us, it seems Honey and I have some wedding plans to make."

Morgan clapped him on the shoulder as he walked

past, and then winked at Honey. Jordan gave her the thumbs-up.

Casey yelled, "Hey, Dad, just so you don't change your mind, I'm calling Grandma to tell her!"

Sawyer paused. "Now? It's not even dawn yet."

Gabe smirked. "And you know damn good and well she'd skin us all if we waited even one minute more."

Sawyer laughed. "Hell, yes. Go ahead and call her. But you can answer her hundred and one questions, because I don't want to be interrupted." He smiled down at Honey and squeezed her tight. "I plan to be busy for a long, long while."

HARLEQUIN
Temptation.

Cowboys.
Every boy's hero...every woman's fantasy.
They can rope, they can ride...
But can they change a diaper?

What happens when three intrepid cowpokes bravely go
where none of them had ever *dreamed* of going before—
the nursery!

Find out in **Vicki Lewis Thompson**'s
wonderful new miniseries...

THREE COWBOYS
AND A BABY

Temptation #780 *THE COLORADO KID*, **April 2000**
Temptation #784 *TWO IN THE SADDLE*, **May 2000**
Temptation #788 *BOONE'S BOUNTY*, **June 2000**
and
Harlequin Single Title, *THAT'S MY BABY!*,
September 2000

Don't miss these tender, sexy love stories,
written by one of Harlequin's most beloved authors.

Available wherever Harlequin books are sold.

HARLEQUIN®
Makes any time special ™

Visit us at www.romance.net

HT3COW